THE SPURLOCK GUN

THE SPURLOCK GUN

by

Matt Logan

Dales Large Print Books
Long Preston, North Yorkshire,
BD23 4ND, England.

British Library Cataloguing in Publication Data.

Logan, Matt
    The Spurlock gun.

    A catalogue record of this book is
    available from the British Library

    ISBN   978-1-84262-782-2 pbk

First published in Great Britain in 1998 by Robert Hale Limited

Copyright © David Whitehead 1998

Cover illustration © Gordon Crabb by arrangement with
Alison Eldred

The right of David Whitehead to be identified as the author of
this work has been asserted by him in accordance with the
Copyright, Designs and Patents Act, 1988

Published in Large Print 2010 by arrangement with
David Whitehead

Dales Large Print is an imprint of Library Magna Books Ltd.

Printed and bound in Great Britain by
T.J. (International) Ltd., Cornwall, PL28 8RW

For the purtiest little
schoolmarm in the east

ONE

Chase Donovan was as drunk as a fiddler's bitch.

Again.

Every evening for the past three days, he'd stumbled into the Deuce of Hearts Saloon, bought a bottle of Old Pepper from his dwindling bankroll and retired to a corner table to ease the hurt inside him, and at closing time every night one kindly soul or another had carried him back to the flophouse where he'd taken up residence since quitting the Ranger barracks to the west of Del Rio, cussing an unjust fate.

Of course, there'd been plenty of times in the past when he could've used the sweet burn of good Kentucky bourbon at the end of an especially rough mission in some God-forsaken corner of the state, but he'd always fought the temptation because he'd been a Texas Ranger, and Texas Rangers were supposed to be men that other folks looked up to.

But not any more.

On this fourth evening, he reached for the bottle and tilted it with a belligerent, unsteady hand, watching with hungry eyes as red whiskey filled the thick-bottomed shotglass. And why not? The star-in-the-circle was gone now, history. For the last three days he'd been *ex*-Texas Ranger Samuel 'Chase' Donovan, so there was no longer any need to keep a clear head, to be in control, to take care never to leave himself open to his enemies.

He closed long, tanned fingers around the glass and raised it slowly to his bristly, waiting lips, hesitating momentarily before taking that first sip of the night because, in its way, it was still as momentous and symbolic a gesture as it had been the first time – the breaking of a self-imposed rule he would never have even *considered* breaking were he still a part of the Special Battalion.

At last he threw back half the glass, savouring the taste on his tongue before swallowing.

There.

It was good. *Real* good. But sourly he reminded himself that it was about the only good thing to have come his way this week.

It was seven o'clock in the evening and, as had become his custom, he'd staggered along to the shack-town district that occupied the outskirts of Del Rio in order to dampen down the rage that still threatened to tear him apart. Even packed as it was with serious drinkers like himself, however, the Deuce of Hearts was a cheerless place, patronized mostly by footloose men who no longer had any true purpose in life save trying to forget what had brought them here in the first place. Still, the games were straight and they didn't water the whiskey, and those facts alone were enough to convince Donovan that it was a good, safe place for a hurting man to lick his wounds.

All right – so they'd thrown him off the force. So what? It was their loss, not his. But still he missed the weight of the badge on his dust-powdered, waist-length denim jacket.

Dammit!

He needed another drink to deaden the pain.

There…

Just as he started pouring a refill, a big black man pushed in through the squeaky batwings and propped for a moment, letting his gaze pan slowly from right to left above the heads of the other patrons.

The man was about forty, with big features and eyes like flaked gold. He stood well above six feet in height and was muscular with it. He dressed range-style, but he didn't strike the former Texas Ranger as a cowboy. The holster and shell-belt around his waist were too well-kept for that, and so was the fancy .45 with ivory grips that sat in the pocket.

At last, apparently satisfied with his surroundings, the newcomer pointed his spur-hung stovepipes toward the bar, moving with an easy, measured stride.

Sobering briefly, Chase watched the black man settle one foot on the tarnished brass rail, heard the soft tinkling of his spur chains, the gentle slap as he set a coin down on the counter and asked for an apple brandy. He was clean-shaven, had a dark, glistening skin, a broad nose and thick, unsmiling lips. Beneath his high-crowned grey Stetson he looked to be bald.

There was something about the man that made Chase feel somehow ... *edgy*.

Aw, but what the hell...

Drunk as that aforementioned fiddler's bitch, he allowed himself the luxury of indifference. Why should he care if the man was trouble? Horse-thief, feudist, road-agent, cattle-lifter ... 'far as he was concerned, that feller could do or be whatever the hell he liked. Wasn't any of his beeswax one way or the other.

To hell with them all!

Another drink and he forgot all about the

13

black man, although the anger continued to simmer and nag inside him. Well, that figured. Like his badge, the meeting he'd had with Captain Taylor three days earlier was history now, but it was fresh enough in his mind that he was still smarting from it.

The damned meeting, and the home truths he'd been forced to confront at it...

'Come in, Chase. And shut the door behind you. I reckon you know what this is all about.'

Heeling the door closed, the tall Ranger had swept off his curl-brimmed, sweat-marked Montana peak hat, crossed the functional, adobe-walled office and dropped into the ladderback chair on the visitor's side of Taylor's desk without waiting to be invited. If he really *did* know why he was there, the wind-burnt face beneath his shaggy, black-turning-grey hair gave nothing away.

He was handsome in a rough, knocked-about kind of way, his features hawkish, eyes a cool, mocking green. Long in the leg and powerfully but compactly built beneath a red cotton shirt and buckled chaps worn over faded and much-mended black denim pants, he appeared relaxed and easy, but the Ranger captain knew that this was just a façade. In reality, Chase Donovan was like a coiled spring ... only in Donovan's case, the spring was just about ready to snap.

'I'll come straight to the point, Chase,' Taylor said abruptly. 'I want your badge.'

The green eyes squeezed to slits. 'Say *what*, captain?'

'You heard. You went too damn' far this time, Chase, broke just about every law there is to break on that little shivaree of yours down into Mexico. You must've known there'd be hell to pay for it.'

But even as he said it, Taylor wondered how you could expect a man like Donovan to consider the consequences of *any* action. He was too all-fired impulsive for that. At just a little past thirty-four he was still relatively young – but already he'd been a law unto himself for too long. He was an old-style peace-officer who believed that the minute he broke the law, an owlhoot gave up any rights to which he might otherwise be entitled.

Well, that was the rough-and-ready way they'd always done things in the past, before the country went and got itself civilized. But times – and more importantly, *attitudes* – had changed. Donovan's kind of lawman – all six-guns and muscles – was a vanishing breed now, and in Taylor's opinion that was no bad thing.

Still, there was no denying that the man got results. A hundred-thirteen arrests in eight years was a hell of a record. But to get those arrests he'd had to shoot more than forty men, killing fifteen. And that wasn't counting all the ones he'd brought in nursing broken arms, legs, noses, ribs–

Nauseated, he stopped cataloguing, but was fair enough to allow that the list of injuries cut both ways. Chase himself had been on the receiving end often enough. Shot twice, stabbed twice, stuck with lance and arrow and beaten from pillar to post more times than anyone could remember, and all in the pursuance of his duty.

But right now that was beside the point. This latest shenanigan had brought things to a head, and the *jefe de rurales* down south had lodged an official complaint with the Governor, who was just about ready to spit rust over it.

'Got anything to say in your own defence?' he asked.

'Only that I was just doing my job,' Chase replied.

Taylor snorted. 'Your job was to apprehend Laredo Kane – and the job ended the minute he slipped across the border and out of our jurisdiction.'

Chase curled his lip. 'Kane was a lying, cheating, gun-running murderer,' he said in a low Texas growl, 'and you know as well as I do that he's been playing us for the fool long enough. We've been after him for what, ten, twelve months? But every time we get close, the snaky sonofabitch rides south, where the law says we can't touch him. Well, this time I was no more 'n a day behind him, day and a half at the most. You expect me to turn around and let him get away, *knowing* I'm so close, just because he pulls that God-damn border-crossin' stunt again? Hell with that!'

Taylor let the air out through his nostrils. 'For God's sake, Chase, how many times do I have to say it? The minute you crossed that line, you stopped being a Ranger and became just another *gringo*, and that's the top and bottom of it. Now, I know damn' well who Kane was, he was everything you say and more – but the fact remains that you had no authority to go busting into a crowded cantina with your .44 blazing away. Christ Almighty, what if you'd killed a bystander in the overspill?'

'I didn't. And just to keep the record straight, it was Kane who started shooting first, not me.'

'Oh, I'll just bet it was, the minute he saw who it was coming after him,' Taylor retorted.

18

Chase stiffened. 'What's that supposed to mean?'

The captain's face went flat. 'It means you've overstepped the mark once too often, Chase. You've picked up a reputation.'

'Repu–? What kind of reputation?'

'The wrong kind,' Taylor replied harshly. 'The kind a man gets when he becomes a little too fond of using his gun, or his fists, or that damned Bowie blade that hangs from the back of your belt. The kind he gets when he'd sooner shoot first and ask questions later.' He hesitated a moment, then finished quietly, 'The kind a man gets when he starts to scare the good guys as much as the bad.'

Chase made an impatient gesture with one hand. 'I do my job,' he bit back. 'That's all you need to concern yourself with.'

'Doing your job's one thing. I've got plenty men out there who do that. But *you*...'

He let the sentence hang, because the facts spoke for themselves. In fact, the Kane business was a perfect example. All right, maybe

Chase was right, and Kane had started shooting first. But whose fault was that? He should've known better than to brace Kane in such a public place, quite apart from the fact that he shouldn't have been anywhere near Mexico to begin with.

Even then, of course, he might have been able to pull it off and no real harm done. If he'd only waited, picked his moment, made his collar and got Kane out of there nice and quiet... But patience never had been Chase's strong suit. To Taylor's way of thinking, he was just a blunt instrument, a means to an end. Once you put him on a case he became obsessive, would pursue his man from hell to breakfast in order to make his arrest, and damn the consequences.

That's why he'd had to blast hell out of a crowded cantina before he could put Kane down, risking serious injury or worse to more than thirty innocent bystanders. Why he'd had to shoot the local headman in the arm when the poor, confused bastard tried to stop him from leaving town with the body

– and why he'd been forced to cross sixty miles of Mexican badlands one step ahead of a fighting mad patrol of the *Guardia Nacionale* before he could reach the safety of the Rio Grande's northernmost shore.

Without warning he said, 'Let me ask you something, Chase. You got any friends around here? A girl?'

'What's that got to do with anything?'

'*Have* you?'

Making another impatient gesture, the Ranger murmured, 'No girl.' And pinning Taylor with the green glare of his eyes, he added pointedly, 'No one I'd really call a friend, either.'

Taylor shook his head, almost in pity. 'No. Just your gun and your star. And that's where you've gone wrong, Chase. You've let the job become your whole life.'

'Is that so wrong?'

'Every man should have a life outside of his work, helps him keep things in perspective. But you ... it's like you're on a crusade, Chase Donovan out to clean up the Lone

Star State single-handed. But what have you *really* achieved, Chase? Where has it *really* got you?'

Donovan's teeth, very white against the sunburn of his face, clenched. Good question. Where *had* it got him? All he had to show for his eight years as a Ranger was his name, 'Chase' – which he'd picked up back in '81, after pursuing two bank bandits name of Magoffin and Bayliss two hundred and fifty miles from Eagle Pass to Gainesville, up near the border with Indian Territory.

'I could dress it up for you, tell you it's nothing personal, just that the Mexicans are pushing to make an international incident out of what you did unless we punish you ourselves,' Taylor continued. 'And that'd be true enough, 'far as it goes. But instead I'm giving you the whole of it – that I got no need of a man like you anymore. You've done the job for too long. It's become part of you, *all* of you. It's clouding your judgement … and I don't need a man with clouded judgement in the Battalion.'

He held out one hand, palm up. 'The badge?'

Through anger-tight lips Chase said, 'Does this come right from the top, or is it just you who's decided I've had my time?'

'It comes right from the top, Chase. 'Fact, if I hadn't fought it for as long as I have, you'd've been thrown out long before this.'

Well, that was straight enough, he guessed. At least he knew where he stood now. Nodding, Donovan got to his feet and tugged on his hat. As he did so, sunlight reflected off the nickel star pinned to his jacket and sent a sunflower-yellow reflection skittering across the room's plain white walls. 'All right,' he growled. 'You want the badge, you can have it.'

He tore the star free but didn't hand it to Taylor, he just threw it onto the paper-heavy desk that sat between them, where it made a solid, chunking sound.

'So long, captain.'

'Chase?'

Donovan stopped at the door, looked back

with one eyebrow raised.

Taylor said, 'For what it's worth, I'm sorry. But you knew this was coming sooner or later. You couldn't carry on the way you were and expect to get away with it forever.'

Chase narrowed his eyes. *Get away with it?* Taylor made enforcing the law sound almost like a crime itself … and maybe that's just what it was becoming in these so-called 'civilized' times. Looking at it that way, maybe he was better off *without* the star.

'So long, captain,' he said again. 'See you around – maybe.'

And here he was four days later, boozed-up, washed-out and still burning with anger and resentment because what Taylor had said had stuck in his mind and made him take a long, hard look at his life.

He hadn't realized it before, but the job had become everything to him. And now that he no longer had it, he was nothing. How the upholding of the law had come to occupy his entire existence he couldn't say.

Somehow it had just … *happened.* Maybe it had something to do with the fact that he'd always been a loner. Perhaps throwing himself into the job had been easier than trying to forge friendships. He just didn't know.

Bitterly he grabbed up the bottle again but tried to rebel against the need to drink before he started to pour. *No.* The liquor wasn't solving a single damn' thing. And in any case, the bottle was just about empty. Briefly he thought about buying another, but decided against it. The whiskey wasn't working anyway, not really. He might as well go on back to his lodgings and try to sleep it all away.

A shadow darkened his table and he looked up through bleary eyes. A man in a blue shirt and pin-striped pants held up with suspenders was standing beside his table. Chase squinted up at him, trying to place him because he looked vaguely familiar. A moment later his sluggish brain told him it was the Negro who'd pushed in through the batwings earlier on, the apple brandy drinker who'd made him feel edgy.

The black man smiled fleetingly and said, 'Mind if Ah join you?'

He started to pull out a chair on the other side of the table but stopped when Chase slurred, 'Matter of fact, I *do.*'

The black man looked at him through his curious flake-gold eyes. 'You Chase Donovan, am Ah right?' he said. His accent was unmistakably deep south, Alabama or possibly Louisiana.

Chase nodded tiredly. 'Yeah, I'm Donovan. Now go take a hike.'

'Sooner have a talk with you, iffen that's all right.'

'It's not.'

'Too proud to talk to coloured folks, mister?'

Chase gestured to the bottle. 'Too drunk,' he replied.

The Negro looked into his bloodshot eyes, saw the truth of his words and nodded slowly. Wasn't much point talking to the man while he was so likkered-up. 'Awright, Mr

Donovan,' he said, lifting thick brown fingers to the brim of his Stetson. 'Some other time, mebbe. Sorry to've troubled you.'

And without another word he turned and shouldered his way effortlessly through the crowd and back to the bar, leaving Chase to frown after him, curious but too damned drunk to do anything about it.

'Sides, he had a date with a shuck mattress.

He pushed to his feet, held to the edge of the scarred table for a handful of seconds until the noisy, foggy room stopped spinning and he felt confident enough to risk trying to walk unaided to the slatted doors. When he shoved out into the darkening night a minute or so later, he propped gratefully beside a porch-post and let the gentle southerly wind cool the sweat on his face.

For a few seconds he just stood there, listening to the sounds of revelry coming from the saloon behind him and all the other, similar establishments that occupied this run-down section of town. They were good, warming, comforting sounds – the laughter of men and the clink of their glasses, the occasional, fun-filled scream of a soiled dove and the odd tinklings of badly-tuned pianos. The few men moving along the boardwalk paid him little attention. An ancient wagon trundled past on greaseless, protesting wheels and the batwings behind him swung open as another handful of patrons left the Deuce of Hearts.

At last he turned left and started wide-stepping clumsily back to his lodgings, but before he'd covered six feet he sensed a sudden stirring of movement directly behind him and started to turn as one unseen hand closed on the butt of his .44 and yanked it from leather and another fastened on his knife and tore it from the beaded sheath at the small of his back.

'Wha–?'

The muzzle of his own gun was rammed into his spine and a voice close to his ear grated, 'Keep movin', you sonuvabitch.'

'Who–?'

'Just keep movin', I said!'

He did. But with every pace he tried to sober up and place the voice. Did he know it? Hell, that surly kind of rasp could've belonged to any one of a hundred men, a *thousand!* He kept walking, breathing hard and fast in the hope that it might help him to shrug off the effects of the whiskey, and as he did so he listened to the sounds of their boots striking the warped planks underfoot because, among other things, he needed to know how many of them there were.

He figured three.

A narrow alley came up on their left and the pressure of the gun-muzzle shifted from his spine to the sensitive flesh just below his right ear. The same voice growled, 'Down here,' and he turned into a pool of inky blackness that was relieved only by the cold white light of the full moon high above, cursing every drink he'd taken today and which had left him open to these men ... whoever in hell they happened to be.

They walked on for maybe twenty yards,

the pace slowing a little as they picked a more cautious path between sacks and boxes stuffed with stinking garbage, and then a high plank wall that closed off the far end of the alley told Chase that they'd evidently reached their destination.

The man wielding his gun pushed him and he stumbled forward, somehow managed to get his legs tangled in the broken remains of an old chicken coop and slammed to earth with enough force to raise a cloud of dust. Three shadows fell across him and he thought, *I was right, then. Three of 'em.*

He rolled slowly onto his side and squinted up at them, seeing them for the first time. Licking his lips, playing for time, he said, 'Do I know you fellers?'

The one holding his gun said, 'Nope. But I reckon you know my brother, Grant Devlin, well enough. You gut-shot him on the Staked Plains a year ago last July ... an' now you ain't got a badge to hide behind nomore, I've come to make you pay for it.'

TWO

Chase's cool green eyes narrowed dangerously.

Grant Devlin, he thought. *Yeah.* Road-agent with a preference for stage hold-ups and a habit of shooting anyone who didn't jump to do whatever he said. Devlin – sick in the head, never happier than when he was scaring hell out of everyone else. Cruel. Violent. Unpredictable.

Chase had trailed him to a wide place in the road called Flynn Springs when he progressed from larceny with violence to outright murder, but somehow Devlin had got to hear about it and lit out for points north before Chase arrived.

The general feeling around town was that Devlin was hoping to lose his pursuer in the wilderness of the nearby Staked Plains. He might've done it, too, because there weren't many men who'd brave that wilderness, what the Mexicans called the Llano Estacado, if they could help it. It was a great swathe of stinking-hot, Comanche-infested desert-land, largely treeless and dry as a bone, a mean, killing country that men shunned if they had any sense.

Chase had kept right after him, though, and that more than anything else had enraged Devlin, made him stop running and turn back the way he'd come in order to gun Chase from ambush and get the Ranger off his trail for good and all.

It was his bad fortune that what should have been a killing shot was made too soon and went wide of the mark, but that was as nothing to what happened in the donny-brook that followed. Devlin caught a bullet in the stomach, but it didn't kill him out-right. So, when it became obvious that he couldn't be moved, Chase had had no choice but to fort up in that flameless hell and wait for the killer to breathe his last.

It took longer than he'd thought it would.

Devlin hadn't died easy, and it hadn't been easy to watch him sink and hear his pleading screams and feel powerless to do anything about it ... until that third day, when he knew he couldn't ignore what had to be done a moment longer.

That third day, when he took out his .44 and put the barrel to Devlin's fevered temple and clenched his teeth and pulled the trigger, showing Devlin more mercy than he'd ever shown any of his victims.

Yeah, he remembered Grant Devlin, all right.

Chase worked up some saliva and spat off to one side. Now that he came to study on it, the Devlin before him now, this vengeance-hunter, didn't look unlike his brother. Same pock-marked skin, glossy black hair, spiteful blue eyes. Only difference was, this one was older and, if such a thing were possible, meaner.

His companions were of an age with him, late thirties, tall, two of them narrow-hipped, the third considerably beefier. Devlin, the one who was holding his .44 and had his knife tucked behind his belt, was clean-shaven, dressed in a creased orange shirt and brown corduroy pants. Chase's eyes dropped fleetingly to his waist, saw that he carried his .45 in an angled, quick-draw holster.

The second man was bearded, in a blue shirt, black pants and a long, bottle-green riding jacket, his sidearm nestled in the pocket of a fancy black leather holster that was decorated with silver studs. In the stark moonglow Chase saw a round face with seamed, nut-brown skin, and dark brown eyes that showed a willingness – no, more than that, an *eagerness* – to inflict pain.

The third man was also bearded, wore a crimson bandanna at his throat and had his yellow slicker folded back so that he could get to the .38 in his cross-draw rig quickly if he needed to. He had shaggy eyebrows and a drinker's nose that looked more like a lump of uncooked dough in the centre of his sun-flushed face.

The Devlin brother made a gesture with Chase's long-barrelled .44 and said, 'Get up, Donovan. I been waitin' a long time for this.'

Slowly he got his feet under him, heard their quickened breathing, sensed their building excitement, knew there was no way he'd ever talk them into changing their minds about the thing they'd decided to do.

Well... He'd lost his job, and like Captain Taylor had said, the job had become everything to him. Take that away and there wasn't a whole lot left. Which meant...

Which meant that he didn't have a whole lot to lose–

He went into action at the same time they charged him from three sides, blocking Devlin's first punch and dodging a haymaker from the man in the red bandanna. A hard fist smashed into the side of his head from the right – that was the third man, the biggest man, the man he thought of as Silver Studs – and his hat went spinning as stars popped inside his skull.

The Old Pepper had already shot his balance to hell, and the blow to his head did nothing to improve it. He slewed sideways, collided with Devlin and they crashed into all the garbage piled up in front of the plank wall.

Chase landed on top and took full advantage of the fact, batting Devlin's hat away, grabbing a fistful of the man's long, glossy black hair and cracking his head against the rutted hardpan. Once, twice, a third time, with Devlin grunting each time his skull met the ground.

Then a boot took him in the ribs and he slammed against the shuddering plank wall. Another kick followed almost immediately, but this time he caught the boot 'twixt toe and heel and twisted violently, heard a yelp and saw Red Bandanna spinning away with his arms working like windmills.

Chase came up just as Silver Studs cannoned into him, shouldered him back against the fence and started pummeling his midriff with fists like small hams. Face screwed out of shape at the pain of it, Chase cupped his hands and cracked one against each of his opponent's ears, and as Silver Studs howled at the stinging agony of it, Chase butted him in the nose and that made him squeal and swear even more.

Another kick flung him sideways, this one from Red Bandanna. Pain exploded inside him, forced the air out of him in a groaning rush. He collapsed in a heap and two men crowded him in, just silhouettes against the deep purple of the star-spattered sky.

Instinctively he folded his arms over his face and head, brought his knees up to protect his belly, curled into as small a ball as he could manage and tried to weather the storm of kicks and blows that followed.

The next minute passed as slow as treacle, and then he heard Devlin's rasping voice again, coming between hungry gulps of air, saying, 'Get him up … let me at him…'

As the other two fell back, panting hard, Chase – bloodied, bruised, wanting to puke up all the whiskey swilling around inside him – glanced up between hooked fingers, caught the spill of moonlight off the object in Devlin's right hand and felt his guts clench reflexively.

The bastard was going to use his own Bowie blade on him.

'Get him up!' Devlin hissed impatiently.

Hands grabbed him, yanked him back to his feet, and he moaned softly without wanting to as he came erect. *Aaaahhh...* They'd damaged his ribs, broken them maybe, but still he fought them, cussing a blue streak as he kicked Red Bandanna in the shin and made the bearded man howl.

Red Bandanna let go of his arm and he lashed out at Devlin with the improvised weapon he'd retrieved from all the trash – an empty can with the jagged, open lid still attached.

He swiped at Devlin's face and Devlin screamed high like a startled woman. Before Chase could really enjoy his moment of triumph, however, Silver Studs clouted him alongside the head again and little pearls of light flared behind his eyes. While he was still staggering, the big man struck at his arm and the blood-smeared can dropped from nerveless fingers.

Rough arms grabbed him again as he shook his head to try and clear it, and the next time he opened his eyes, Devlin was standing right in front of him, his pocked face a twisted mask of rage, blood dribbling from a three-inch hairline cut just beneath his left eye.

In a low, dangerous voice, Devlin said, 'I'm gonna carve on you now, you sonuva-bitch. I'm gonna carve on you an' then I'm gonna cut your heart out while you is still screamin'–'

Before he could do any such thing, however, the alleyway was filled with the ratchety *cli-cli-click* of a handgun coming to full cock, and a low, southern voice hissed tightly, 'No you ain't, mister.'

As if by some mutual, unspoken agreement, Devlin, his two companions, even Donovan himself, stopped moving, almost stopped breathing, for not even the harsh sawing of their labouring lungs sounded in the confines of the alley now.

Then, slowly, Devlin turned, stood back so that he was no longer blocking Chase's line of vision.

The Negro from the saloon was standing spread-legged at the mouth of the alley, his fancy .45 with the ivory grips held easily in his right fist, the short blued barrel centred rock-steady on Devlin's chest.

Devlin squinted at him, searched quickly for any sign of authority but found none. Still holding the knife, he said a little uncertainly, 'What business you got pointin' your damn' smoke-wheel in my d'rection, feller? We' jus' settlin' a little private dispute down here, tha's all. Ain't nothin' to you.'

The black man just looked at him, his face wide and unreadable, and even at that distance Chase could see that his dark lids had dropped down over his flake-gold eyes to give him an edgy look. With iron in his tone now, the black man said, 'Drop that blade, mister, an' all you fellers take your pistols from leather an' throw 'em yonder.'

Still no one moved. Lips were licked, fingers flexed, chances weighed by men to whom trouble was a way of life.

The black man said, 'Ain't goan tell you again, you sumbitches. Now, you do like Ah say.'

'You,' Devlin snarled in reply, 'go to *hell!*' And he dropped the knife and clawed for the Colt at his hip.

A gunshot slammed its flat, ugly thunder along the alley and Devlin shrieked, threw his pistol away, hugged his right arm to his narrow chest and bent double. Beside him, his two companions froze in the act of reaching for their own guns.

Down at the far end of the alley, smoke curled leisurely from the barrel of the black man's Colt. He said, almost gently now, 'You do like Ah *say*.'

At first no-one moved. Then hands dropped more slowly to gun-butts and weapons were eased carefully from holsters. In the centre of the knot of men, Chase backhanded blood off his chin, swayed back and forth and drew in warm night air as the alleyway cartwheeled crazily around him and his battered ribs kept stabbing away.

The guns dropped into the garbage with heavy iron thuds. Devlin muttered, 'My *wrist* … bastard's busted my wrist!' He sounded like he was having trouble believing it.

Ignoring him, the black man said, 'Now you men get outta here, outta town. Ah lays eyes on any of you again, Ah won't bother none with no mo' fancy trick-shootin', Ah'll jus' shoot t'kill. You got that, you fellers?'

There was some shuffling of boots, the soft sound of Devlin still whispering, 'Bastard's busted my *wrist!*' Red Bandanna nodded eagerly.

'Now *git,*' said the Negro.

Helping Devlin, the other two hustled along the alleyway, anxious to please. The black man stood to one side to keep an eye on them, and they all but scraped their backs against the far wall as they edged past him.

'*Bastard!*' snarled Devlin, speaking through

teeth that were clenched against pain.

Unmoved, the black man only said, 'You better get that there hand seen to afore you quit town.'

As the sound of their bootfalls diminished, Chase lowered himself slowly to his knees in order to retrieve his knife and pistol. The effort made him wince, breathe hard, want to puke again.

The black man came striding down to him, his movements almost graceful, his spur-chains setting up soft music that ended when he halted above the Ranger-turned-drunk. Chase raised his face and, still bleeding from the mouth, said, 'That was a … pretty … piece of gunplay, mister.'

The .45 spun briefly in the black man's hand before vanishing back into its holster. 'Wasn't displeasin',' he replied. 'You all right, feller? You lookin' awful pale.'

'I'll … live.'

'Well … happen you ain't feelin' too aggrieved, you think we might have that talk now?'

Chase said fervently, 'Mister, I'm all ears.'

But even as he said it his eyelids began to flutter … and a moment later he passed out and fell flat on his face at the black man's feet.

For a long time after that there was only darkness. Darkness, and memories of the life he'd led and which had brought him to this low point.

He'd been born just outside of Ballentine, on the Colorado River, in 1853, the only son of mostly indifferent parents. His father – a big, ruddy-faced man who liked beer and cards a little too much for his own good – had inherited a small, hardscrabble farm several years earlier, but had little real understanding of the land and even less interest in it. One failed crop after another, coupled with an unwillingness to do anything to improve the situation, had put him ever deeper in debt with the bank, so times had been lean and Chase – just plain Sam as he'd been called back then – guessed that had been much of the reason for his parents' resentment of him, because his had been one more mouth to feed when they could least afford it.

When the bank finally foreclosed, the Donovans moved into Ballentine. His father tried his hand at a succession of jobs, but the persistent and irresistible lure of beer and cards saw to it that he rarely held one down for more than a month at a time.

Pa went to war in '61 and died at a place called Missionary Ridge two years later. In the meantime, a succession of strange men had taken to visiting his mother in the evenings, and during one of the rare times when she actually bothered to speak to him she told him they were his uncles, but of course he knew that they weren't uncles at all. It wasn't that his mother was a libertine, he would never allow himself to think that. It was just that times were hard and she had to earn a living somehow.

Still, it was no kind of life for an eleven-year-old boy to have to witness, so one dark night he helped himself to a few cold-cuts from the pie safe and went on the drift.

He travelled right across the state, earning money whenever he could find one menial job or another, and stealing food to fill a growling belly whenever he found himself flat broke. That's where he'd really learned to prefer life as a loner. Things were a whole lot simpler when you had no one but yourself to look out for.

He'd gone six years living like that, drifting, working, stealing, and then stealing more than working because it took less effort. Then he got himself arrested on a vagrancy charge in the town of Catch Creek, just across the Rio from San Antonio de Bravo, and his punishment – if you could call it that – was a twenty-four hour stay in jail.

Lord, that had been the best twenty-four hours of his life! A roof over his head, a decent, home-cooked meal taking the pleats out of his belly and, for the first time, someone to talk to, who really seemed *interested* in him.

Marshal Ed Spurlock.

Spurlock, as he was later to learn, was one of the great peace-officers, firm but fair, gun-swift when the situation needed it but with a kindly nature too. He'd left a wife and son back home up in Amarillo someplace while he fulfilled what he hoped to be a short-term contract to bring law and order to Catch Creek, and though he never spoke much about them, it was plain that he missed them both real bad. Maybe that's why he took such an interest in the younger man, because he reminded him of the boy he had up north.

To this day, Chase still remembered that stay in jail, Spurlock's long, lined face studying him through the strap-steel bars, his soft, persuasive voice reaching out to touch something hitherto untouchable inside the young drifter.

'The State needs good men, Sam. It's still tryin' to get over a war that's torn it asunder, and it needs every good man it can find. You understand what I'm tellin' you, boy? I'm tellin' you that anyone can go bad. Hell, that's easy. But it takes a special kind of man, with a special kind of strength, to stay good, honest and upright. I reckon you got that kind of strength. But I'll tell you plain – you could still go bad iffen you don't make a real effort to straighten yourself out afore you get much older.'

And Spurlock had helped him do just that, had taken him on as a turn-key and paid him from his own pocket, and the more he'd seen of the law and its workings, the more Chase had come to realize that his own future lay in the upholding of the law.

He had finally found his purpose in life.

Sensing as much, Ed had talked the town council into giving him Chase as a deputy, and he'd learned everything there was to learn about enforcing the law from the lean-flanked town-tamer. But the old restlessness was still in him. As much as he enjoyed the work, as much as he revered Spurlock, who became more of a father to him than his own father had ever been, he just wasn't one for the routine of town life.

Ed had sensed that too, suggested one day that if he *really* wanted to stay in the badge-packing business, he could do worse than ride southeast to Del Rio and try his luck with the Rangers.

He did. And for eight years the Rangers had been his entire life. But then one day he got word that Ed had been killed trying to stop a robbery at the First Bank of Catch Creek, stopped seven bullets, left a grieving wife and son behind him ... and something inside Chase had snapped at that, turned colder and meaner and more obsessive.

From that moment forward he'd gone after the bad guys with a vengeance...

Without warning, he woke up.

'Uhnn...'

Mouth dry, head pounding, vision blurred. Mind still cluttered with dreams and half-memories, none of which made any sense. Maybe he was ill or something.

No, no, not ill ... just hungover.

He slowed his breathing, tried to calm his churning stomach, and presently his vision cleared enough for him to take a closer look at his surroundings.

The first thing he saw was a display of flowers, greeting him cheerfully from a vase on a bedside cabinet, and his whiskery lips curled because he'd always hated flowers.

Aside from that...

He was in a large bedroom, in the bed, and late morning sunshine was flaring whitely at the wide, curtained window. He looked around, noting the ornate, upholstered Belter furniture, the delicate chamber set on the sideboy, the gas lighting, the plush carpet. Somewhere in the lower regions of the house he heard people talking softly, and doors opening and closing.

Everything about the place spoke of money, and that was no description he'd have ever used on the flophouse where he'd so recently taken up residence. So where the hell was he?

Brief flashes of recollection tantalized him.

A Negro, carrying him effortlessly across one brawny shoulder, shoving through a group of onlookers who'd been drawn to a dark alley by a single gunblast... And now, creaking and rattling, something hard beneath him – a wagon-bed? – and the dark, star-spattered Texas sky above.

He'd been taken somewhere, then. In a wagon. And presumably, against his will.

He closed his eyes again, willed the memories to come faster, clearer...

They did.

Still flat on his back, but in a real bed this time – *this* bed – and people looking down at him and hissing gaslight spilling into his eyes, hurting them. An older, jowly man with a stethoscope dangling from his neck, speaking with a tired, slightly bored voice.

'Cuts ... grazes ... considerable bruising to the body. This man was roughed up by experts, Mr Kissing.'

Eyelids drooping now, as the man – doctor? – taped him up. He remembered fighting another wave of unconsciousness, looking from the jowly man to the Negro, from the Negro to–

Oh Jesus.

–to the woman.

Tall, slim, in her mid-twenties. Hair a tawny mass, swept back from a clear, tanned face to cascade in soft, shining, curls down her back. Direct brown eyes, deep, intelligent, determined. A straight, tip-tilted nose, pronounced cheekbones and a full, confident mouth, pinched down now with concern–

Seeing her again in his mind stirred something inside him that went 'way beyond simple desire, and the instinctive longing he felt for her, a woman he didn't even know, shocked and confused him.

He closed his eyes again. He was sweating, trembly. But he had a million questions that needed answering, and he wanted them answered *now*. Determinedly he threw back the covers, sat up slowly and eased his legs over the edge of the bed. He was naked except for the bandage that bound his ribs.

He stood up. He had to find out where he

was, who had brought him here – and why. First, though, he had to find his clothes.

They weren't hiding. They'd been piled on the chair beside the dressing table, and they'd all been freshly laundered. Even the busted stitching on the shoulder of his denim jacket had been repaired.

On his way to get them, he paused at the window, partly to see if he could get any clue as to where he was and partly to draw in deep, reviving draughts of clean morning air. All he saw were rolling hills and lines of shade trees, and here and there great crescents and oblongs of flowerbeds.

Flowers!

As he grabbed for his shirt, he noticed his holstered Army Colt on the dressing table itself, the buscadero shell-belt, from which hung the beaded sheath that held his big, bone-handled Bowie knife, wrapped protectively around the pocket, and sight of the weapon only confused him more, because even though there was no evidence to support the claim, he couldn't shake the conviction that he was a prisoner in this place.

He dressed as quickly as his injuries – and his hangover – would allow, and was just tucking the faded red shirt into his black pants when he heard the door behind him swing open.

His right hand blurred to the Vulcanite grips of his .44 and the Colt left its pocket in a whisper of steel. He pivoted and dropped to a crouch, the .44's long barrel a flashing arc of blue light in front of him.

The woman froze in the doorway, her eyes wide and her red mouth describing a perfect O. He noticed that she was wearing a trimly-tailored powder blue dress that covered her from neck to ankle.

Sight of her threw him temporarily, and he faltered briefly before recovering himself. When he spoke, his voice was a harsh snapping that struck at her like a series of slaps.

'Where am I?'

'I… Please, Mr–'

He came up to his full height. 'Where am

I? Why did you people bring me here?'

'Please, I–'

'*Tell me, dammit!*'

As she opened her mouth again, a shadow moved in the hallway behind her and one carpeted floorboard gave the slightest creak. Immediately his green glare shifted from her now-pale, almost triangular face to a point beyond her – and the barrel of the Colt did likewise.

A second later the Negro appeared behind the woman, hatless now and, as Chase had suspected, as bald as an egg. Without taking his eyes off Chase, he said calmly to the woman, 'S'awright, ma'am. Ain't nothin' to worry 'bout here.'

He slipped through the door and put himself in front of her, and a rare smile moved his wide mouth. 'Be obliged iffen you'd put the gun away, Mr Donovan. You' frightenin' the lady.'

Chase only grated, 'Where *am* I?'

'You' among friends,' the Negro replied. 'That's why they's no call to go brandishin' that there six-killer. 'Sides, it's empty. Ah took the bullets out just after we arrived las' night.'

'You sonofabitch!'

'Seemed like a sensible precaution at the time,' replied the black man.

'Who are you people?' Chase rasped. 'What the hell am I doing here?'

'Ah don't blame you for wantin' some answers, Mr Donovan. Ah would, too, iffen Ah was in your boots – which Ah was, oncet. You hungry?'

But the former Ranger was damned if he'd let himself be sidetracked so easily. 'For some answers, sure.'

The Negro hesitated a moment, then nodded as if affirming something to himself. 'Awright, Mr Donovan. You want answers, and sho' nuff you' entitled to 'em. Leather yo' weapon … an' then we'll see what we can do to satisfy yo' curiosity.'

THREE

Chase backed away from the Negro, reefed up his gunbelt and hurriedly buckled it on. Cautiously, half-expecting some kind of trick, he said, 'All right – lead on.'

Before he did so, however, the black man surprised him again by sticking out one hand. 'Name's Kissin', by the way,' he said. 'Jonah Kissin'. This here is Miss Lydia.'

Chase made no move to take the hand, said instead, sceptically, *'Kissing?'*

Amusement showed fleetingly in the black man's flake-gold eyes. 'Brother,' he replied, dropping the proffered hand without rancour, 'ain't nothin' you can say 'bout it that ain't already been said.'

He turned and indicated that the woman, Lydia, should precede him out of the room, and the minute he turned his own back,

Chase thumbed open the loading gate on the side of the Colt and started punching in shells from the loops on his belt.

Only when the gun was loaded with five cartridges, and the hammer was resting on the empty sixth chamber did he allow the knots in his gut to slacken off.

Grabbing his disreputable Montana peak from where it hung slantwise on the chair-back, he followed Kissing and the woman out into a long, wide hallway, grimacing when he saw the fancy little bowls of flowers that graced every ornate table, window sill and recessed shelf he passed.

At last they reached the head of a staircase with intricately carved mahogany ballusters and followed it down past a run of expensive-looking oil paintings in gilt frames, heading for the ground floor. Like everything else about this place, the sun-bright reception area below was impressive and spoke of money. A wide front door was flanked by two tall windows, more paintings, more heavy, high-priced furniture and yet more bowls of flowers. He could hardly stand to breathe for all their cloying fragrance.

Two Mexican servants, a man and a woman decked out as butler and maid, followed their descent. Their eyes were big and nervous. Addressing the maid, Lydia said briskly, 'Ynez – breakfast for our guest, *por favor.*'

Chase's eyes narrowed. *Guest?* He didn't feel like much of a guest. And yet these people had done him no real harm. Just the opposite, in fact. All they'd done so far was save him from almost certain death, patch him up, wash him down and generally take care of him.

Jonah Kissing reached a set of double doors at the far end of the reception area, rapped briskly against one of the panels and then swung them wide to reveal a large room with a high ceiling.

Chase hesitated a moment, instinctively getting the layout of the place fixed in his mind in case he needed to get out or seek cover fast. A moment later he warily followed Kissing and the woman inside.

The room was long and bright. The left-side wall was shelved from top to bottom, and each shelf was crammed with books. Circular sofas and overstuffed chairs were dotted around the big fireplace opposite, and up at the far end, to one side of curtained French windows that were ablaze now with noonday sunshine, stood a row of polished wooden file cabinets and some map drawers. The room had apparently been furnished to act as a combination study and office.

Directly in front of the French windows sat a vast, blocky desk inlaid with red leather. A man in a grey suit, white shirt and maroon cravat was sitting at the desk, pen in hand, blond head bent over a stack of documents. As the woman closed the doors behind them he looked up, set the pen aside and gave Chase a frank examination from out of pale blue eyes that, even from this distance, Chase could see were old before their time.

He said, 'Ah, Mr Donovan. I've been

looking forward to meeting you. How are your ribs feeling this morning?'

He was in his late twenties, of surprisingly slight build, with a narrow, clean-shaven face and short, fine, side-parted fair hair. He had a bookish look to him – just what you'd expect of a man who shared his life with so many of the damn' things – and a sore look to the rims of his eyes.

'I'll live,' Chase replied in a growl. In fact, they hurt like a bitch.

'Man wants to know where he is, an' why he's here,' said Kissing, lowering his big, graceful body to one of the red velvet sofas.

'And who *you* people are,' the former Ranger added grimly.

The man behind the desk sat back, still appraising him. 'All right, Mr Donovan. First things first. You're at my home just outside Rocksprings.'

Chase ran the name through his mind. Rocksprings. Forty miles from Del Rio, or thereabouts. Kissing must've driven that wagon through half the night to get him here.

No wonder the doctor had sounded so tired: they'd obviously called him out in the small hours.

'That's the *where*,' he said. 'Now let's hear the *why*.'

Something in the blond man's eyes sharpened and he put his elbows on the desk and steepled his long, artistic fingers. 'Word has it that you just lost your job,' he said. 'I wanted to offer you another one. That's why Jonah was in Del Rio last evening, searching for you. And lucky for you that he was, the way I hear it.'

'Seems to me you hear a lot of things, mister.'

'Sometimes it pays to keep one's ear to the ground,' the blond man allowed. 'Take you, for instance. I've heard all kinds of things about you over the years, Mr Donovan. And I've made it my business to follow your, ah … exploits, shall we call them? Deputy Marshal, Texas Ranger… You have a record to be proud of, by and large, and I'm impressed. In spite of your sometimes heavy-handed and not always entirely justified methods, you have a healthy respect for the law, I think, and you're about as incorruptible as any man is ever likely to be.'

Chase only sneered. 'Why don't you just get to the point?'

The blond man's smile was thin. 'All right, I'll say it once and I'll say it plain. We might be heading towards the last decade of the nineteenth century, but that doesn't mean we're any more civilized or law-abiding now than we used to be. Lawlessness is just as rife now as it ever was, maybe even more so. And I'm not just talking about the west, I mean right across the country. The US Marshal's office, the Rangers, the Pinkertons, the Secret Service, the Army – they're all being stretched to breaking point, and they need all the help they can get. That's why we need someone like you, Mr Donovan. Someone ... flexible ... who can work outside the law in order to enforce it.'

Chase eyed him sidelong. 'You want to hire me to do what I've been doing ever since I pinned on a badge?'

'That's it *precisely*. You and Jonah together will be my own private lawmen. You'll go where I send you and settle the problems the law is either unaware of, turns a blind eye to, or is powerless to deal with. You'll be well paid for your trouble, I guarantee it. There is just one proviso, and without it we have no deal.'

Chase said insolently, 'Is that a fact?'

'It's a fact you can bank on in Denver,' the blond man replied solemnly.

'All right, let's hear it.'

'I'm not stupid, Donovan. I'm enough of a realist to know that you'll be fighting fire *with* fire out there. But I will not tolerate your maverick attitude and needless brutality any more than the Rangers did. So you will have to mend your ways if we're to get along as well as I hope we will. You'll have to go back to being the kind of lawman you *used* to be.'

Chase snorted. 'Who the hell're you to start preaching to me, mister?'

'I'm the man who's offering you the

64

chance to keep doing what you do best –
fighting for law and order. Unless, of
course, you'd prefer to go back to the Deuce
of Hearts Saloon?'

Ignoring that, Chase growled, 'And what
do *you* get out of it, while I'm dodging all
the bullets?'

'You wouldn't believe me if I told you.'

'Try me.'

The blond man glanced briefly at Lydia,
then shrugged. 'If you insist.'

But the woman interrupted him. 'Let me,'
she said, and there was steel in her voice
when she addressed Chase. 'I imagine that
even a man as blunt and unpleasant as you
once had a father, Mr Donovan. Did you
get along with him? Admire him?'

He didn't meet her gaze. 'Not so's you'd
notice.'

'Well Andrew *did*,' she continued. 'Oh,
don't worry, I'm not going to give it to you
with violins. But Andrew's father meant
everything to him, *everything*. All he ever
wanted to do was follow in his footsteps, to

65

do what he did, and tame this wild country.'

Chase glanced back at the blond man, Andrew. 'What stopped you?'

The other man's shrug was filled with resignation this time, and a moment later he reached down below the desk ... and started dragging at the wheels attached to either side of his chair.

He backed up and then wheeled himself around the desk, his legs looking bent and withered beneath his grey trousers and, surprised, Chase's expression slackened a notch until the old stubbornness came back and hardened it up again. After all, the blond man didn't want his sympathy any more than he felt compelled to give it.

'This is what stopped me,' Andrew said without any trace of complaint or self-pity. 'A stagecoach crash when I was six years old. My legs were crushed ... and this is the result.'

Chase glanced meaningfully around the room. 'You seem to have made out all right,' he remarked.

'I can hardly complain. I might have lost the use of my legs, but I was blessed with a certain ... talent ... for playing the markets back East, and making vast sums of money. So, as you can see, I am able to live in relative comfort.'

Chase put it all together fast. 'So because you can't follow in your father's line of work, you want to do the next best thing and hire it done?'

'Now,' said the blond man, 'we understand each other.'

Chase's mind raced. A chance to get back into law enforcement–! On the surface at least, this was the answer to a prayer. But he still wasn't totally convinced. He didn't know these people and wasn't sure how far they could be trusted. He'd be taking a damned risk, and no mistake.

'Well, Mr Donovan?' asked Lydia.

He looked at her and wanted her and hated himself for it, because she was the one soft thing that had ever come into his life, and that made him stop, and think, and question … and Chase was a man of action who didn't like to think any more than he had to.

'I hope you'll say yes,' she continued. 'It would mean so much to Andrew.'

His eyes dropped to her hands, knitted together now just beneath the swell of her breasts, and his mouth compressed when he saw the wedding band on her finger. She was married, then, doubtless to this Andrew. Married, and thus unattainable. And yet still he wanted her, *needed* her.

He said impatiently, 'You people're crazy,' and turned to head for the door, and seeing him go she spoke again, hurriedly this time.

'Perhaps it would help to know exactly who my husband's father was,' she said. 'You might find that you have more in common with him than you think.'

He broke stride, hesitated a moment, then turned slowly back to face them, these crazy people. What she'd said, and the way she'd said it, sent a chill down his face. He looked from the woman back to Andrew, one raised eyebrow asking not for an answer, but for confirmation of what was already going through his mind.

The man in the wheelchair said, 'Yes, Mr Donovan. I am Andrew Spurlock. My father was *Ed* Spurlock.'

Ed Spurlock... The name all but rocked him back on his heels. No wonder the son wanted to follow in his father's footsteps! Ed had been enough of a man to inspire *anyone*.

Andrew Spurlock said, knowingly, 'That makes a difference, doesn't it?'

Chase thought, *Of course it does.* To enforce the law was one thing, a high and honourable thing. But to enforce the law in the name of the man to whom he owed everything, and maybe repay something of the debt ... that meant infinitely more.

And then, of course, there was Lydia. If he stuck to his guns, told these people no and walked out of here now, that was *it*. He'd never see her again.

He told himself that he was still hungover

and not thinking straight, that she was just a woman, no different to any other, and he should know better than to act like a love-lorn fool.

But these people were waiting for his answer. They were giving him a unique opportunity to carry on doing the only thing he was good at. And it wasn't as if he had anything better lined up.

Ed Spurlock…

'Tell you what I'll do, Spurlock,' he said roughly. 'We'll give it a go, just one job. And I handle it the best way I see fit. If it doesn't pan out, or I don't get results, we each go our separate ways and no hard feelings.'

Andrew's smile was broader this time, warmer, and it brought vitality to his old man's eyes. 'And if it *does* pan out?' he prodded.

'If it pans out,' Chase sighed, wondering what the hell he was letting himself in for, '…you just hired yourself a gun.'

'The *Spurlock* gun,' murmured Lydia.

From a distance, the town of Willow Bend was just a haze of grey dust rising towards the washed-out scorch of blue Texas sky. A little closer and it took on more detail, became sun-faded clapboard dwellings and busy hardpan streets, false-fronted stores and peeling log pens filled with bleating cattle.

The land around Willow Bend was lean and cheerless – just red earth and buffalo grass, low sandhills and ravines and occasional stands of dogwood and maple. Fifty miles north lay the border with Indian Territory, and not even half that distance separated the town from the Panhandle country to the northwest.

A cattle trail passed close by, however, the one they called the Western, and as men in big hats and dusters and chaps pushed their herds ever north from San Antonio to Fort Buford, in the Dakota Territory, a distance as near as dammit to a thousand inhospitable miles, they too had to pass within sight of the town ... and to men starved of company and comfort and fun, the grey haze that pushed toward the cloudless sky looking mighty inviting.

Willow Bend was a cow-town, then, and the confusion of casinos and saloons and whores' cribs that clung to its northern fringes offered the cowboys all the fun they could possibly want – for a price. And prices were high in that latter-day Sodom. Only life was cheap in the red-light district of Willow Bend.

And therein lay the town's problem. A problem Andrew Spurlock's two personal lawmen rode in to solve a little over a week later.

Because there was no direct rail route through to Willow Bend, Chase and Jonah had to make the long journey north by way of a series of unreliable spurs and feeders that took them as far as Padgett. There they caught the stage to Seymour, and in Seymour they bought horses for the saddles they'd lugged with them, a coppery sorrel

and a seventeen-hand blood bay respect-
ively.

During that final push north, Chase finally
broke his long silence to ask Jonah how he'd
come to be recruited by Spurlock.

The way he explained it, Jonah had been
busting broncs for a liveryman in Compton,
East Texas, when a Saturday-night fight
broke out between rival brands at the only
saloon in town. When the marshal tried to
break it up, however, the whole drunken
pack had turned on him and likely would've
killed him but for Jonah's intervention.
Unable to simply stand by and watch like all
the other townsfolk present, he alone had
waded into the mêlée, cracking heads with
the butt of his distinctive handgun until
reason returned to the likkered-up mob.

Spurlock had come to hear of it, and,
believing Jonah to be just the kind of man
he'd been looking for, had quickly sought
him out. Since Jonah had already decided
he was getting too old and too shook-up for
horse-breaking anyway, he decided to give

Spurlock's proposition a go. As a one-time soldier, he was used to taking orders, and as a former Wells Fargo shotgun guard, he knew how to handle a gun. He said he'd been travelling the state for the last seven months, handling fairly routine matters for his new boss.

Now they had an experienced lawman on the team, however, Spurlock had decided that the time had come to handle something a little more … *ambitious.*

The blond man hadn't been kidding when he'd told Chase that he kept his ear to the ground. In fact, he'd deliberately cultivated a network of informants to act as his eyes and ears right across the country. The minute they saw or heard anything they thought he might be interested in, they sent him a telegram about it, and then Spurlock and Lydia put everything together before deciding whether or not to get involved.

That the system worked well was borne out by the comprehensive briefing Spurlock had been able to give them regarding the

Willow Bend case. At the end of it, Andrew had also suggested they introduce themselves to the town marshal, Tom Fry, upon their arrival. Once they'd convinced him of their good intentions, Fry could then bring them up to date on any new developments.

Chase was impressed – although he would never admit to it. The more he saw of Andrew, the more he saw of Andrew's father in him. The blond man didn't brood on the ill fortune that had stolen away the use of his legs, he just got on and made the best of things. He could be quietly-spoken, charming and polite ... but he could also be ice-cool and single-minded. Most of all, however, he shared Chase's own contempt for those who flouted the law.

Given time, the two of them might even have struck up a friendship of sorts if Chase hadn't been such a loner, that was.

And if it hadn't been for Lydia.

The long journey to Willow Bend gave Chase plenty of time to think about the woman, and to start doubting the wisdom of having accepted Spurlock's proposition in the first place.

Lydia was still an enigma to him, aside from what he'd been able to learn about her from Kissing – that she'd come west from Kansas City, Missouri, had married her husband four years earlier and was completely devoted to him. If that truly was the case – and Jonah had no call to lie about it – then he realized now that seeing her with the man she loved was going to hurt him even more than never seeing her again.

For that reason, he decided to stick to his side of the bargain and see this first mission through to the finish – but then do what he should have done right at the outset ... to put her from his mind and ride on.

They entered town from the south, walking their mounts in through the noisy, dust-shrouded cattlepens, and then reined in at the far end of Main to take their first real look at the place.

Willow Bend had been built on a grid system, with three wide streets running north-to-south and another three bisecting them east-to-west. The widest street ran straight through the middle, and that was Main.

Main was bustling. It boasted a goodly selection of stores, as well as a couple of restaurants, a hotel and a bank. Saddle-horses stood patiently at tie-racks or heads dipped to water troughs. Wagons with shuddering canvas awnings trundled heavily over the ruts in the dusty road. Shielded from the worst of the hammerblow sunshine, men, women and children ambled along the covered plank boardwalks, and here and there, wilting shade trees did their best to keep pointing skyward.

Jonah nudged his high-crowned grey Stetson back off his sweat-beaded forehead and said, 'Don't look like much wrong with this town to me.'

Chase only shrugged, easing his back after the long ride. According to Spurlock, Willow Bend was a town ruled by violence, intrigue and intimidation.

'Tell you what,' he replied, thumb-scratching his jaw. 'You go book us a couple rooms at the hotel and I'll go hunt up the marshal.'

The Negro nodded, reached out one big paw. 'Here, gimme yo' reins, I'll stable th'hosses, too.'

As Chase watched him lead the animals away, he wondered just how he was going to get along working with a partner. Previously, he'd always worked alone. He preferred it that way … and realized now that his fellow Rangers had likely preferred it that way too. Well, it was only going to be for the one mission. He figured he could grin and bear it for that long.

He turned away from Jonah and scanned Main Street again, this time searching for the law office. It was right where he expected to find it, directly opposite the bank, about three-quarters of the way further down the street, a squat, solid, brick-built structure one storey high, its heavy strap-oak door reached by three crumbling stone steps.

A couple of minutes later he twisted the

handle and let himself inside. It was appreciably cooler in there, dimmer too, and it smelled of stale coffee and even older paperwork. As he closed the door behind him, he scanned the single, wood-panelled room, saw two scarred desks, a file cabinet, weapon rack and a pot-bellied stove upon which sat a blackened coffee pot. Another door in the facing wall more than likely led through to the cellblock.

A man was seated behind one of the desks, hands cupped behind his head, legs up on the desk and crossed at the ankles. A dead match protruded from one corner of his narrow mouth. He was no more than thirty, with a big frame, a square face and macassared hair the same shade of white blond as his eyebrows.

Chase said, 'Marshal Fry?'

The man behind the desk said, 'Nope.'

Chase came deeper into the office, his boots making a hollow clatter on the waxed floorboards. 'The marshal around?'

'You're lookin' at him.'

'I thought–'

'Well, you thought wrong, pilgrim.'

Chase studied the man closer, took in the dark unreadability of his brown eyes, the sour line of lips almost hidden by a generous steerhorn moustache, the challenging jut of his square jaw. Most of all, however, he noticed the matched Colts sitting in the cutaway pockets of the man's double gunbelt, .38 calilbre Lightnings with flashy six-inch barrels.

'You got a name, marshal?' he asked.

'Dexter,' replied the man, sliding his spurless heels off the desk so that he could sit up straighter. 'Phil Dexter. *You* got a name, pilgrim?'

'Smith,' Chase replied vaguely. 'What happened to Marshal Fry?'

'Whyfore you askin', *Smith?*'

He wondered briefly if he should say. But something about Dexter sat uneasily with him, and that being the case it was better to say nothing at all. 'Looking for work,' he lied. 'Met a feller on the trail, he told me to look up Marshal Fry when I reached town, said maybe he could point me in the right direction.'

He knew it sounded weak, but there hadn't been any time to come up with anything more believable.

'Well, Fry's gone,' said Dexter. 'An' far as work's concerned, you can always see what's goin' down at the pens.'

'I'll do that.' He made to turn and leave, but stopped at the last moment and offered Dexter a look of puzzlement. 'What happened to Marshal Fry, anyway? Must've quit in an awful hurry.'

'He did,' Dexter replied, getting to his feet and striding closer, his eyes lingering deliberately on Chase's old, sweat-marked hat, the trail-dust powdering his jacket and pants. 'An' so will you, you don't find yourself a job right quick. We got strict laws against vagrancy in these parts … *Smith*.'

Chase should have nodded and told Dexter he'd be no trouble and just got out of there. But the other man's attitude riled him, made him stand his ground all the more. 'You wouldn't be threatening me, would you, marshal?' he asked casually.

Dexter reached up and took the dead match out of his mouth so that he could offer a contemptuous smile. Chase saw that he had small, square, white teeth. 'When you're the law, you can do any damn' thing you please, boy. Iffen you don't like it–'

'Funny you should say that,' Chase cut in. ''Cause I *don't*.'

Dexter's very dark brown eyes seemed to dim at the interruption, and his smile vanished quicker than a short beer. He said in a low voice, 'Well, we'll try real hard not to upset your feelin's for as long as you're here – *Smith*. Now, you jus' go find yourself a job an' keep your nose clean. Happen you can't find anythin' – don't linger 'round here.'

Chase smiled back at him, but with his mouth alone. With a belligerent shrug he made to turn again, until Dexter flattened one palm against his shoulder.

'I *mean* it, boy,' he said quietly, and with

the fingers of the other hand he snapped the dead match in two.

Chase's cool green eyes came back up to rake the lawman's face. He thought, *Bad mistake,* and down at his sides, his fists started clenching. But then, unbidden, he saw her face in his mind. *Lydia.* And he remembered Spurlock's words. *You'll have to mend your ways if we're to get along as well as I hope we will. You'll have to go back to being the kind of lawman you* used *to be.*

He felt the tension leave him. Spurlock was right. A confrontation wasn't going to get him anywhere: leastways, not yet.

Slowly the fists uncurled and, hating even the pretence of backing down, he replied mildly, 'I'll try to remember that, marshal.'

He let himself out quickly, just in case he changed his mind and decked the lawman anyway.

FOUR

Chase lingered a moment outside the office, breathing deep to calm his rising anger. He couldn't remember the last time he'd backed down from *anyone,* and it came hard to do so now.

'Fact, that was another thing about the Spurlock set-up that he didn't like. He did things *his* way, always had, always would, and he wasn't sure he had the patience to practice the kind of restraint Spurlock had insisted on, leastways not when throwing a punch at a gold-plated jackass like Dexter offered so much more in the way of satisfaction.

The small hairs at his nape stirred and he turned his head to see the gold-plated jackass looking at him through the smeared glass of the barred window to one side of the heavy door. Gritting his teeth, he reached up, fingered the brim of his hat in acknowledgement and then crossed the street.

Jonah was propping beside a tie-rack outside the hotel, waiting for him. As he drew nearer, the black man frowned and said, 'You awright, brother? You' lookin' mad as a teased rattler.'

'Forget it. You get us a couple rooms?'

'Sho' did. How'd you make out with the marshal?'

'I didn't. The marshal's gone, lit out. They got a new man wearing a badge now, sonofabitch named Dexter.'

'What happened to Fry?'

'That,' said Chase, 'is anyone's guess. I tried to find out, but if Dexter knew, he sure wasn't telling.'

'So where does that leave us?'

'Well–'

He broke off as Phil Dexter hurried past on the other side of the street, a low-crowned black hat now shading his big, square face. Following his gaze, Jonah narrowed his flake-gold eyes and hazarded, 'That Dexter?'

'The one and only.'

'Looks like a man in a pow'ful hurry to get someplace.'

He did at that, and Chase wondered why. Dexter hadn't looked much like he was fixing to leave his office on an urgent errand before he, Chase, had walked in. Could be he'd made the man nervous with all his questions about Fry. In which case, where was he going in such an all-fired hurry now?

'Mayhaps we should wire Mr Spurlock,' Jonah said as Dexter disappeared around a corner. 'He'll know what to do.'

'*I* know what to do,' Chase snapped tiredly. He was feeling kind of touchy. His bandaged ribs still hurt and he was still mad at himself for feeling the way he did about Spurlock's wife. A split second later, however, he had all the fatigue and anger and discomfort locked up tight again, and said in a milder tone, 'We go grab ourselves a bite to eat, *that's* what we do.'

'An' after that?'

'We find Tom Fry.'

Jonah worked up some saliva and spat into the dust. 'Or what's become of him,' he said grimly.

They didn't have to go far to find an eaterie. There was a well-patronized café right next to the hotel. They went inside, found a corner table and, when the homely waitress came over, ordered buffalo steaks, grits, beans and a pot of coffee.

Just before the waitress turned away, Chase added as if in afterthought, 'Say, ma'am. I hear Tom Fry used to be the law in these parts.'

All at once the background conversation faded, and the waitress lost her pleasant smile and started looking distinctly uneasy. Someone cleared his throat nervously, and in the kitchen out back the cook accidentally dropped a skillet, but they were the only sounds in the sudden silence.

'That's right,' the waitress allowed after a pause, not looking at him.

'What made him quit, do you know?'

Her shrug was more like an involuntary twitch of the shoulders. 'I ... I really couldn't say.'

As she weaved between all the gingham-covered tables to get back to the kitchen, Chase and Jonah exchanged a meaningful glance. The townsfolk occupying the surrounding tables continued to eye them slyly until, gradually, the background buzz picked up again, sounding pretty strained now.

Chase said, 'Still reckon there ain't much wrong with this town?'

Jonah leaned forward as a couple of people got up and left in a hurry. 'Ah'm startin' t'see that there might be somethin' rotten hereabouts after all.'

A little while later the waitress delivered their meal and hustled away before Chase could ask her any more questions. More than ever, he felt that they had to find out what had become of the former marshal, if for no other reason than that he was about the only person in town they were certain they could trust. For sure, they couldn't do much until he brought them up to date with any new developments.

The food was good and there was plenty of it. As soon as they'd eaten their fill, Jonah paid the tab and they headed for the hotel, determined to get some answers *somewhere*.

Five minutes later, however, they were back out on the boardwalk, and Jonah was shaking his head. 'Ah don't like this one li'l bit, brother. Minute Ah mentioned Fry's name, th' clerk's face jus' closed right up. He warn't sayin' no more'n anyone else around here.'

Jonah thought for a moment, then said, 'Newspaper office should have all the answers.'

'Always supposing a town like this runs to its own newspaper,' Chase replied sceptically.

'Oh, it do,' Jonah said with unshakeable confidence. 'It's called the *Willow Bend Advocate*.'

'How'd you know that?'

He gestured casually with one big arm. ''Cause their office is right across the street.'

Chase looked that way and saw it for the first time, a small, dim, glass-fronted structure squeezed between two larger stores, the name of the paper painted on the glass in fancy gold scroll, and beneath it the further legend, PRINTING DONE TO ORDER.

They crossed to the far boardwalk together. An open copy of the latest *Advocate* had been taped to the window for the perusal of passers-by, and its headline screamed:

GUNFIGHT AT THE GLASS
SLIPPER LEAVES THREE DEAD
Honesty of North Town Games
Brought into Question
By Tragedy

Jonah opened the door and they went inside.

A stack of copies of the newspaper sat at one end of a counter that ran the width of the narrow building, and behind it, at a bench upon which sat a galvanized tub, a man in a green apron and sleeve protectors was using solvent to scrub ink off a blackened, smooth-stone slab filled with type. Another man, shorter and heavier, with a big moustache and a dead pipe clamped between his lips, was sitting at a desk, scribbling words onto a sheet of paper. Bundles of newsprint were stacked everywhere, and an enormous printing press, all wheels and trays and rollers, blocked out whatever sunlight might otherwise have brightened the place from the backyard.

A tarnished brass bell sat on the counter. Chase hit it with the palm of his hand and the man at the desk looked up. He was in his middle fifties, with thick, uncombed grey hair and wire-framed glasses.

He looked at Chase first, and then his magnified grey eyes shifted to Jonah. He got up slowly, threw the pen down and came over to his side of the counter, his movements cautious and wary. He was in his shirtsleeves, and his string tie hung loose at his unbuttoned celluloid collar. Chewing the pipe over to one side of his mouth, he said, 'You want something?'

Chase nodded. 'Information.'

'What kind of information?' the man asked.

'Trying to find your old marshal, Tom Fry,' Chase explained. 'Seems to be a hard man to track down.'

'What's your interest in Tom?'

Chase gave him a cool smile. 'That's *our* business, mister.'

'Well, I'm sorry, but all I can tell you is that Tom Fry left these parts a couple weeks back, moved right out of the state. Settled himself someplace up in the Indian Territory, as memory serves.'

Jonah cursed under his breath, but Chase gave no reaction at all. Instead he asked, 'You the editor of this paper, mister?'

The grey head nodded once, a very definite, proud assertion. 'John T. Setright,' the man replied. 'Owner, publisher, editor-in-chief.'

'I guess that makes you a pretty upright

citizen then, Mr Setright – but I still think you're lying through your teeth. I think you know full-well where we can find Marshal Fry, but you just ain't saying.'

The man who was washing the ink-stained slab in the background stopped what he was doing and looked around. John Setright's lips firmed up around the dead pipe and his glasses magnified the hostility that suddenly flooded his eyes. In a voice that shook with anger, he said, 'I think you'd better leave.'

'Listen, mister, we need to find Fry.'

'Oh, I'll just bet you do. But he's gone. You people scared him away for good. Isn't that enough?'

Sensing that they might finally be getting somewhere, Chase opened his mouth to ask another question, but before he could get started he heard the sound of a gun coming to cock and Setright brought a six-shot, double-action Adams .442 up from beneath the counter. His face was absolutely expressionless now, and all the more dangerous because of it.

'I said you men had better leave,' he repeated.

Taking a chance, Chase said, 'You're mixing us up with the wrong outfit, Setright. We're here to *help* Fry.'

Setright's jaw muscles clenched and unclenched rapidly as his anger continued to build. *'Help* him? Oh, sure. Help him into an early grave! For God's sake, haven't you bastards done enough damage? Now go on, get out of here before I forget that I don't ordinarily condone violence!'

He stabbed the .442 at Chase, and the gesture made both of Spurlock's enforcers take an involuntary step backward. Raising his palms, Jonah said, 'Awright, mister, awright. You done made yo' point. We's goin' now.'

He backed to the door and opened it by touch, not daring to take his eyes off the gun in the newspaperman's fist. Chase followed suit, but hesitated in the doorway. 'You change your mind and decide to believe us,' he said, 'we're staying at the hotel across the street.'

'Just get the hell out of here!' stormed Setright.

They got.

They *got* pretty much the same reception everywhere else they went, too. Jonah returned to the livery, ostensibly to check on their horses, and found the livery man ready and willing to shoot the breeze ... until Marshal Fry's name came up in conversation. Chase met with the same reaction when he asked after the man at the barbershop.

As the long afternoon finally waned, Chase returned to the hotel, collected his key from the frosty clerk and climbed the stairs to his room. It was a clean-enough first-floor front that opened out onto a gallery that overlooked Main.

Because his ribs were still paining him, he unbuckled his gunbelt and measured his length on the bed. The heat was sapping, and the long afternoon's thankless toil had only added to his fatigue. Still thinking about the missing Tom Fry, he fell into a light doze.

A soft rapping at the door woke him two hours later. He sat up, reached for his .44 and called, 'Who is it?'

'Me,' said Jonah.

He got up, went over and unlocked the door. Jonah came in with a brown-glass bottle of apple brandy in one hand. As Chase closed the door behind him he said, 'Any luck?'

'Nary a murmur. You?'

Sliding the long-barrelled Colt back into leather and lifting the funnel on the oil lamp so that he could light the wick and scare some of the early evening dusk away, Chase shook his head.

Jonah took off his hat, threw it on the chair beside Chase's Montana peak, flopped down onto the crumpled bedspread and held out the bottle. Chase automatically declined, still thinking the way he had when he was a Ranger, that you had to set an example. But hell, there was no one around right now, and a shot of brandy might help to sharpen his thinking even more.

He reached for the bottle and took a pull from the neck. On the bed, Jonah said, 'Like it or not, Ah still think we oughta wire Mr Spurlock. Could be he's picked up on somethin' we haven't.'

'You just hang fire on that idea,' Chase warned. There was no need to involve Spurlock yet. Christ, it was still early days yet, they'd only just arrived in town. 'I'll think of something.'

'Such as?'

Handing the bottle back, he walked across to the window. 'There's still one place we haven't tried yet,' he muttered. 'North Town.'

'North Town', so they'd learned, was the name given to Willow Bend's red-light district by the locals.

'When do we go, brother?' asked Jonah, sitting up and setting the bottle on the bedside cabinet.

Chase was already reaching for his gun-belt. 'Right now,' he replied.

Before they could go anywhere, however,

there was another knock at the door. Jonah came up off the bed as Chase crossed the room and, standing to one side of the door, said, 'Yeah, who is it?'

There was a pause, and then a muffled voice said, 'Setright.'

Chase threw a quick, over-the-shoulder glance at his partner. So – the newspaperman had had a change of heart. Without thinking about anything else, he opened the door–

–and found himself staring down the octagonal barrel of the newspaperman's English-made pistol.

Setright said gravely, 'Don't move. Don't say a word. Don't even *breathe*.'

He jabbed the pistol at Chase and Chase backed into the room, hands automatically rising to shoulder level. Setright came in and behind him came two other townsmen, a big, bearded man Jonah recognized as the local blacksmith, and a younger, slimmer man with *storekeeper* written all over him. All three were brandishing handguns.

The storekeeper kicked the door shut behind them and, at a gesture from Setright, the blacksmith stamped across the room and tore Jonah's .45 from leather. At the same time, the storekeeper placed himself between Chase and his gunbelt.

There was a moment of silence then, as everyone surveyed everyone else. Then Chase broke the spell, saying with deceptive ease, 'Hello, Setright. Changed your mind about talking to us, I see.'

Beneath his big grey moustache, the newspaperman curled his lip. 'By God, you're a cool one,' he murmured. Then, without taking his eyes off Chase or Jonah, he addressed the blacksmith. 'Bert, give 'em their hats.'

'We goin' someplace, mister?' asked Jonah.

'Earlier on you came to my office looking for information,' Setright replied in a soft, dangerous tone. 'Well, now it's my turn.'

'Can't we, uh, talk here?'

'No,' breathed Setright. *'We can't.'*

The storekeeper moved back to the door and opened it, and Setright gestured with his head that Chase and Jonah should leave ahead of him. Around them, the hotel seemed unnaturally quiet, as if the staff and guests were deliberately keeping out of the way, and the feeling was reinforced when they descended the stairs and found the reception desk empty, the frosty clerk nowhere in sight.

Chase slowed down, trying to think of a way to turn the tables on their captors while they still had the chance. He didn't believe they were in any real danger, but if a man was desperate enough... Well, there was no telling for sure. A jab in the small of the back from Setright's gun kept him moving, and together they went out onto the deep blue street, where five horses were waiting at the tie-rack, among them Chase's sorrel and Jonah's big blood bay.

'Mount up,' snarled Setright. 'And no tricks.'

Yet again they did as they were told, and a minute later, with Setright leading the way and the storekeeper and the blacksmith flanking them on either side, they left town at a canter.

There was no further dialogue. They rode west in silence, across a darkening plain that was splashed with blue and white columbines and studded with grey-boled cottonwoods. After about forty minutes, Chase spotted lights up ahead and judged them to mark the windows of a low log cabin. As they rode nearer, the moonlight picked out a small and largely unremarkable ranch.

Slowing their horses to a walk, they clattered into a dirt yard that was bordered by a big, slant-sided barn, an open, empty wagon shed and a peeling, weathered bunkhouse. The place looked run-down and deserted but for the yellow-white lamplight that showed inside the cabin.

Setright, a man unused to riding, reined in and dismounted stiffly. He handed his reins to Bert and then marched up to the cabin, while the storekeeper told the prisoners to, 'Get down and lead your horses into yonder barn.'

They did just that, and tied the animals to the slats of the first stall in line, then waited while Bert found the closed lantern and struck a match. As butter-coloured light blossomed and spread, it revealed shaggy bales of hay and stacked tools, a couple of wall-eyed horses and a pile of dusty old flour sacks. A few minutes passed in near-silence, and then Setright appeared in the big double doorway, accompanied now by another man.

This man was of average height, with the beginnings of a belly pushing against the buttons of his blue nankeen shirt. He was in his late forties, with sad grey eyes, a seamed, sun-browned face and a black longhorn moustache that was shot through with grey. He was holding a cut-down Greener shotgun in his fists, with the butt braced against his hip, and his expression said he just couldn't wait to use it.

Aside from the stamping of the nervous horses and the rustle and scurry of disturbed rats, it grew very quiet inside the stale, manure-smelling barn.

Kicking his way through a carpet of straw to get to the other side of the structure, Setright leaned against a saddle-tree and said, 'All right. I said I wanted information, and that's what I intend to get. And you'd better not play me for the fool, either of you, or so help me, I'll gun you down where you stand.'

FIVE

'For starters,' he barked, 'just exactly who *are* you men?'

'My name's Donovan, Chase Donovan, and this here's my partner, Jonah Kissing.'

Setright eyed Jonah doubtfully. *'Kissing?'* he repeated.

'Who sent you here after Marshal Fry?' asked the storekeeper, a tall, underweight man in his middle thirties who had cropped brown hair and a long, clean-shaven face.

'A man named Spurlock.'

Setright frowned, running the name through his mind and coming up empty. 'And just who's this Spurlock? Why should he have sent you here? What's *his* interest in Willow Bend?'

'Let's just say he's a believer in fair play. When he sees something that doesn't set right with him, he sends us out to help even things up a tad.'

'What makes him think we need help?' asked the shotgun man, a little too quickly.

'For years now, you people've made your money off the herds that come up along the Western Trail,' Chase replied. 'But times are changing, and so are the ways the cattlemen use to get their herds to market. Give it another year or two and the Western'll be dead, and so will your town. If you're to survive, you've got to bring new people and new business to Willow Bend ... but before you can do that, you've got to clean up North Town.'

Setright glanced from Bert and the storekeeper to the shotgun man, then said tonelessly, 'Go on.'

Chase shrugged. '"Clean up North Town". Easy to say. But you people're pretty much on your own out here. You can't even call on the sheriff's office to help you out, because you're still living in a county that's only half-settled and barely incorporated. So the only way you can clean up North

Town is to introduce your own ordinances against running crooked games and the like. Once you've got the laws, you can enforce 'em. But to *get* the laws, you've got to hold a ballot and vote 'em in.'

'Trouble is,' Jonah continued, 'North Town's grown too big, too powerful an' too damn' greedy to let that happen. All them saloons an' gaming houses, brothels an' dance halls an' whores' cribs down there, they know's well as you do that time's running out, only they' not taking the long view, the way you are – they just plan to squeeze as much as they can out of them drovers afore they move on. That's why they' fighting you ever' inch of the way.'

'What's that supposed to mean?' barked Setright.

'It means you've awready held one election to get yo' ord'nances made law,' said Jonah. 'But them North Town bullies, they done scared away half the voters an' fixed it so's the rest'd vote the ordinances out. We right, mister?'

'You're right,' muttered the newspaper-man. 'As far as it goes. But all that proves is that you, or this Spurlock character, know what's been going on here.'

'Well, we don't know ever'thin',' Jonah countered. 'Like, fo' instance, what happened to Marshal Fry.'

The blacksmith scratched at his beard, clearly trying to decide whether or not to trust them. A big, brawny man with shaggy black hair that hung over his ears, he said uncomfortably, 'The marshal—'

'Bert...' Setright warned.

The blacksmith looked at him. 'Aw hell, John,' he snapped. 'To hell with playin' these cagey games! Let's just lay our cards on the table, huh?'

'We' listenin', mister,' Jonah said softly.

The blacksmith started again. 'The marshal, he was the one who really worked to get these ordinances passed through. An' they weren't much, not really. All we wanted to do was change things so's no one could operate in North Town without a proper permit.'

'And to get the permit…?' prodded Chase.

The storekeeper took over, much to Setright's chagrin. 'To get the permits,' he said, 'the saloon-owners had to prove to the town council that they didn't water their beverages, the gamblers to prove that their games were straight, and the whores to agree to a regular medical examination once every four weeks, just to make sure they were clean and free from disease. The permits cost forty dollars each, and were renewable every six months. No one could operate without one, and anyone found breaking the conditions of issue could be closed down. In addition, we planned to levy a modest tax on all the alcohol shipped into North Town. That was so's we could pay for a few improvements to the rest of Willow Bend.'

It all sounded fair enough. And in the long term it would help to bring a little order to an otherwise-wild section of town by weeding out the more crooked operators. Chase said, 'Go on.'

Bert took up the story again. 'Well,' he

said, 'you've already answered most of it yourself. The North Town bullies queered the vote and thought they'd won. But Marshal Fry sent a letter to the county judge, explaining exactly what it was we were hoping to do here, and had the results of the vote overturned – which left the way open for a *second* ballot.'

'Before that could happen, however,' Setright continued grudgingly, and with no little bitterness, 'the North Towners decided to take the marshal out of the picture. First they set fire to his house on Third Street. Then someone took a couple of pot-shots at him while he was walking his nightly patrol. And when he still wouldn't give in, they sent two men – if I dare call them that – around to rough up his wife, Phoebe. That, more than anything else, really broke the marshal's spirit. He took Phoebe off to someplace safe, but when it came time for him to ride back to town and finish what he'd started...'

Chase could guess the rest. 'He just couldn't face it.'

Setright nodded.

'And you people think we came to finish the marshal off once an' fo' all?'

'It's no secret that Tom Fry hated like blazes to quit and leave the job half done,' Setright answered. 'It stands to reason that the North Towners would still see him as a threat.'

'What about the new man, Dexter?' asked Chase. 'Where does he stand in all this?'

The storekeeper gave a short, barking laugh. 'Judas Priest,' he said, 'it was Dexter and another bastard who roughed up Tom's wife in the first place!'

Chase stiffened. 'Can you *prove* that?'

'Sure we can prove it. Oh, he wore a bandanna to hide his face, both of them did, and they waited till nightfall before they busted into Tom's house and ... and did what they did. But Phoebe Fry knew it was Dexter, all right.'

'How?'

'Have you met Dexter?' asked Setright. When Chase nodded, the newspaperman said, 'Did you happen to notice his left hand? He's missing the tops of his third and little fingers, some machinery accident he suffered when he was younger.'

'Fry's wife noticed the hand?'

Setright inclined his head. 'Not only that, but Dexter likes to chew on matches, and when he's through with them, he snaps them and lets them fall where they will. Bert here did some poking around after it happened, and where he found sign that the attackers had waited for the right moment, he also found five matchsticks, all of them snapped right in half.'

He shook his head in disgust. 'An ambitious man, Phil Dexter,' he muttered. 'Tom Fry took him on when he was nothing more than an out-of-work gun-tough and taught him everything he knows. And when he was all through learning, he decided he didn't want to be a deputy any more, he wanted the top job.'

'So Dexter's in league with the North Towners.'

'I think it's safe to say that he's on their payroll.'

Having digested all that, Chase said, 'These North Towners, are they *all* against your ordinances?'

'Pretty much, to one degree or another.'

'Anyone in particular?'

'Not as far as we can tell.'

'Well, there's got to be at least *one* person organizing all this intimidation. Find him and you'll be making real progress.'

'But how in the hell are we supposed to do that?' demanded Bert. 'Relations're strained enough between us an' the North Towners as it is. It's not like we can jus' go waltzin' in there, askin' questions.'

'Maybe *you* can't. But maybe *we* can.'

'Assuming for a moment that you've been telling us the truth,' Setright cut in sceptically, 'just how do you think you can succeed where we've failed?'

'You want a fair and open vote, right?' Chase replied. 'Well, you'll only get it after you've gotten rid of whoever's organizing all this intimidation.'

'And you'll do that?'

'Uh-huh. But we'll need help, information mostly. That's why we were looking for Fry. Once we know what we're up against, we can go to work.'

'You talk a good fight, Donovan. I'll grant you that.'

'I was a Texas Ranger for eight years, Setright. Jonah here served in the Fifth Cavalry. We're not exactly amateurs.'

'There's just one problem,' Setright persisted. 'I still don't believe you.'

'Well, you jus' wire Mr Spurlock in Rocksprings, get him to confirm what we've tol' you.'

'Or better still,' Chase murmured thoughtfully, 'give us the chance to *prove* that we mean business.'

Setright's magnified blue eyes showed interest now. 'How?'

'You've got to send out a message to the North Towners that you won't be beaten,' Chase replied. 'Kicking Phil Dexter out of office'd be a good start. But there's an even better way.' He paused a moment, thinking fast. 'This Marshal Fry ... you say the North Towners broke his spirit. But do you think he'd come back and finish the job if me and Jonah got rid of Dexter and then backed him right the way through the next election, like deputies? Be real encouraging for your people if he did.'

The townsmen glanced at each other un-certainly. The near-silence was a palpable, uneasy thing. At length the shotgun man cleared his throat and answered for them. 'I reckon he might,' he allowed cautiously.

Chase looked at him. *'You're* Fry, ain't you?'

The shotgun man held back a moment, then nodded. 'I'm Fry,' he admitted. 'These men've been hiding me and the missus out here ever since I quit town. I ... I would've gone back sooner but ... well, it's been hard. Them bully-boys, they ... they really shot my nerves to hell, you know?'

Chase nodded. 'I can guess. But I've been

watching the way you hold that shotgun, Fry. Your nerves seem to be holding up well enough now.'

'It's settled, then,' said Jonah. Feeling some of the tension leave the air, he drew in a deep breath and stuck out his right hand. 'Congratulations, marshal. Looks like you just got yo' old job back – an' a couple of unofficial deputies into the bargain.'

Twenty minutes later, by which time they'd agreed a rough plan of action, the three townsmen and their former prisoners began the journey back to town. Before they'd gone more than a hundred yards, however, Chase suddenly shortened his reins and signalled a halt.

Setright, who still had his doubts about the Spurlock men and didn't care who knew it, kneed his mount up alongside and said irritably, 'What th–'

Chase raised a hand to shut him up but Setright ignored it. 'What–'

'*Be quiet, damn you!*'

Silence fell again, broken only by the occasional stamp or snort of one of the horses and Setright, muttering indignantly under his breath. As one they all found themselves listening to the moon-washed darkness, four out of the five not really knowing why. All they heard was the mournful howling of a coyote in the far distance. A few moments later Setright spoke again, impatiently. 'Mind telling us what it is we're supposed to be listening out for?'

Chase forced his muscles to relax. 'Thought I heard another rider out there someplace,' he replied, indicating the south and east. 'Guess I was wrong.'

'*I* didn't hear anything,' Bert remarked helpfully.

'Neither did I,' said the storekeeper, who had finally introduced himself as Ernie Weems. 'But if someone *was* out there…'

He let the sentence fade as he, all of them, started wondering if maybe they'd been followed out from town, and what it might mean if they had.

'Bert,' Setright said grimly. 'Perhaps you'd better go back and stay with Tom and Phoebe for tonight. Just in case.'

'Sure.'

'And be careful, Bert. Good blacksmiths are hard to find.'

With a quick, tight grin, Bert nodded, turned his horse with much hauling of reins and kicking of heels, and rode back the way they'd just come. The rest watched him go, then, at a sign from Chase, continued on their way.

Presently the faint haze of town-lights appeared ahead of them, and five minutes later they entered Main at a walk and brought their horses to a grateful halt outside the hotel. As Chase dismounted, his eyes travelled quickly along the other side of the street. A lamp was still burning at the marshal's barred office window. Good. Dexter was working late.

Setright and Weems headed for the café next door while Chase entered the hotel with Jonah at his heels. The frosty clerk, who was now back behind his desk, seemed surprised to see them, but wisely passed no comment as they strode by and climbed the stairs to Chase's room, where they quickly retrieved their weapons.

'Iffen you got a plan,' said Jonah, slipping his ivory-handled .45 back into leather, 'Ah figger now's the time to let me in on it.'

'Hardly worth calling it a plan,' Chase confessed as he buckled on his shell-belt. ''Sides, I don't figure it'll take more'n one of us to kick Dexter out. You might's well take the rest of the night off.'

'Why, thank you all to hell,' Jonah replied laconically. 'But jus' in case it slipped yo' attention, you is still nursin' some sore ribs, brother. Iffen anyone's goan do the kickin', it oughta be *me*.'

'Appreciate the offer,' Chase replied. 'But I figure I can use the exercise.'

They quit the room and went back out onto the street. A few stores were still open but most of the day's trading had ceased and a balmy kind of peace had settled over Willow

Bend. If you stopped a while and listened, however, you could hear the raucous sounds of North Town carrying on the wind, punctuated every now and then by a wild gunshot, or the tinkling shatter of glass.

'Ah'll see t'the hosses, then, iffen you' sho' I ain't got no place in this,' said Jonah.

With a nod, Chase crossed the street and started up towards the marshal's office, suddenly eager for action. He'd hated like hell to back down from Dexter earlier, and he was anxious to set the cat among the pigeons and really get to grips with the North Town bullies. But more than that he wanted to give Tom Fry the chance to regain his dignity, and to pay Dexter back for what he had apparently done to Fry's wife.

Reaching the law office, he closed his right hand on the door handle and twisted, shoving the door itself open and following it into the lamplit, wood-panelled room beyond. Dexter was sitting at his desk and forking a late supper of bacon and beans up off a plate on a tray in front of him. He looked up as the door opened, and stopped chewing when he recognized Chase.

'Well, well,' he said, recovering nicely from the surprise and tossing his fork aside so that he could reach for a folded napkin. 'Look who it is. The man who likes to call himself "Smith".' He blotted the mouth beneath his big steerhorn moustache, then threw the napkin aside, not once taking his eyes off his visitor. 'I've been meaning to look you up – *Donovan*. I think you and me ought to have a little talk about just what it is you're really doing in Willow Bend.'

Chase kicked the door shut behind him, noticing that Dexter's double gunbelt, with its fancy .38s sitting snug in the cutaway pockets, was hanging from a hook on the coat-rack in the corner, well out of the man's reach. He said easily, 'Sure, let's talk. Only I'll go first.'

Dexter's fine white-blond eyebrows lowered a notch, and the merest suspicion of unease showed in the brown eyes beneath them.

'Oh, don't worry,' Chase went on. 'I ain't got much to say, but what there is, I'll say plain.' He paused a moment, and when he spoke again his voice came as hard as steel. 'Get up, Dexter. Get up, take off that badge and then get the hell out of here. You've snapped your last match in Willow Bend.'

For a moment Dexter looked like he'd been slapped in the face. He opened his mouth to speak but said nothing. Instead he pushed back his chair so that he could rise. As he moved, Chase's eyes fell briefly to his left hand and saw that, as Setright had told him, the lawman was missing the tops off his third and little fingers.

'You're drunk,' Dexter growled, flexing his hands and working his broad shoulders expectantly. 'But drunk or sober, no man takes that tone with me.'

He made a move towards his gunbelt but Chase snapped, 'Don't!'

'The hell you say!'

'Maybe you don't understand,' Chase replied, his voice freezing the lawman where he stood. 'I'm calling time on you, Dexter. You and all your friends in North Town. It's like I said just now. You've snapped your last match around here … and beaten up your last woman.'

Dexter threw one final, hungry look at his gunbelt, doubtless wondering if he could reach it before Chase reefed out his own pistol. Then, suddenly, he lunged forward with his fists buckling up and a roar tumbling off his lips, and Chase came to meet him, crouching low so that he could bury his fist wrist-deep in the lawman's belly.

Dexter folded forward over Chase's extended arm and grunted as the air rushed out of him. Before he could recover, Chase grabbed him by the shoulder of his shirt, ripped him back up and slammed him in the face. The big blond stumbled back, caught himself against the edge of the desk and scooped up his plate, turning and throwing it at Chase all in one motion.

Chase ducked and the plate shattered behind him, the impact sending a shower of beans and bacon fat down across his shoulders. The coffee-pot came next, sailing overhead until it flattened against the wall in an explosion of scalding brown fluid, and in that split second, when he was trying to dodge all the missiles Dexter was sending his way, Dexter himself came at him in another rush.

He tackled Chase waist-high and propelled him right across the room so that they both crashed into the door. Chase moaned as pain from his mending ribs flared through him. But even as Dexter released his hold and tried to back off, Chase forced himself to ignore the pain and grabbed him, held him where he was and brought his right knee up in a short, savage blow.

The knee connected with Dexter's face and he took a wild kind of pleasure from the muffled yell it tore from the other man's mouth. He brought his knee up again for good measure, and this time let Dexter stagger back across the waxed floorboards, moaning nasally and clutching his face.

Dexter hit the desk again and leaned across it, gasping for air. Blood from his nose made tiny pattering sounds as it spotted all the paperwork there. Breathing hard himself, Chase said, 'Let's have … the badge, you … sonof–'

But Dexter wasn't finished yet. Without warning, he pushed himself away from the desk and snatched at the gunbelt hanging on the coat-rack. Chase powered after him and grabbed him by the shoulders, but Dexter turned at the waist, so fast and with such force that Chase was thrown forward and around him.

He crashed into the coat-rack and its central column splintered with the snap of a gunshot as he landed in the corner with Dexter's gunbelt beneath him. Dexter blurred in, kicking and stomping for all he was worth, then bent, twisted his fingers into the shoulders of Chase's shirt and yanked him back to his feet.

Whatever else he might have been, Dexter was a rough-house fighter from way back.

He spun Chase around and slammed his head against the desktop in a string of furious up-down, up-down motions, then slipped his hands from shoulders to neck before Chase could recover his wits. Chase felt the thick, strong fingers tighten around the column of his throat and then began to squeeze, squeeze, *squeeze*...

With one side of his face shoved flat against a sea of paperwork that had cushioned the blows just a tad, he tried to elbow Dexter in the belly, but the other man was so close to him that he couldn't get the leverage. A gauzy red mist came down over his eyes as the fingers clamped ever tighter, but then Dexter released his grip, grabbed him by one shoulder and twisted the fingers of his other hand back into Chase's shaggy black-grey hair. All at once Dexter started hammering his head against the papery desk-top again, and it was plain that he wasn't going to stop until he saw Chase's brains oozing out of his ears.

Even with the paperwork absorbing much of the force of the blows, the pain was tremendous, and it was all Chase could do to keep from blacking out. Blindly, desperately, he reached out across the desk until his fingertips brushed against something cool and hard.

Dexter's discarded fork.

Without stopping to think about it, he closed his fingers around the bone handle, brought the fork up and stabbed it down into the back of the hand that was twisted into his hair. There was just the slightest resistance … and then it went in all the way. Dexter screamed at the shock of it and flung himself back off Chase so that he could cradle his punctured hand in his good one. Chase straightened and spun to face him, saw blood welling up around the tines, then went at him with a roundhouse left, a right, a left and one more right for luck.

Dexter's head snapped one way, then the other. Little pearls of blood arced across the room every time Chase hit him. As he forced the lawman back across the office, his knuckles started to numb up, but still he kept at it, punch, punch, face, stomach, until finally the blond lawman's legs turned rubbery and went out from under him.

At last it was all over.

As he stood above Dexter, Chase sucked air into his starving lungs and tried to ignore the sickly pounding in his head. He'd underestimated his opponent and knew he'd been lucky this thing hadn't gone the wrong way. And even though this was hardly the time for it, he told himself sourly that it was just like him to go bulling ahead without bothering to weigh the consequences first.

He was going to have to do something about that irritating little habit one of these days.

He looked down at Dexter, who was crawling around on his hands and knees in all the spilled food and coffee, not really knowing which way was up. Chase bent, hauled him back to his feet and shoved him up against the door, then ripped the marshal's star off his nankeen shirt. While Dexter's eyes were still rolling, he reached for the fork embedded in the man's hand and yanked it free. Dexter howled some more and clutched his hand and tried not to collapse again.

Chase manhandled him out through the door and threw him down the steps and into the dirt. Dexter made no move to resist. He just didn't have any resistance left in him. There weren't many people around, but the few that were still out and about paused briefly to watch what was happening.

Dexter did some more aimless crawling in the dust, then slowly climbed to his feet and stood swaying in the oblong of lamplight that illuminated his blood-slick face and ratty, unkempt white-blond hair. Chase said flatly, 'You can collect your effects tomorrow, on your way out of town. For now, just get the hell out of my sight, you sorry sonofabitch.'

Bleeding from nose and mouth, hugging his wounded hand to his heaving chest, Dexter glared up at him in angry silence, choosing not to waste his breath on threats, idle or otherwise, simply because he didn't have the breath to spare. He held that murderous glare for another few heartbeats; then, still holding his wounded hand, he spat a mixture of blood and saliva, turned and staggered away.

Chase watched him go, his expression unreadable. A few moments later he heard Jonah hustling across the street to join him, and turned. In passing, a cursory glance told him that Setright and Weems had joined a bunch of onlookers outside the café. They looked a little green around the gills at what they'd seen.

Jonah flashed his teeth in a tight, relieved smile, and indicating the departing Dexter, said, 'Well, you sho' nuff showed *him* where to go.'

Glancing briefly at the fork in his hand, its prongs still stained red with Dexter's blood, Chase allowed, 'You *could* say he got the point.'

Jonah winced at the pun and muttered, 'Ouch.'

In silence they watched Dexter stumble

along the boardwalk, turn the far corner and disappear from sight, and suddenly Jonah's smile was replaced by a frown. 'They's jus' one thing Ah don't understan',' he said. 'Why we lettin' that sumbitch go free? Ah suspicion we'd all be a sight safer iffen he wuz behind bars.'

'Yes,' put in Setright who, together with Weems, had finally come over to join them. 'You should have arrested that devil, Donovan. With Phoebe Fry's testimony, Tom could have charged him with attempted murder.'

Chase spared the newspaperman a fleeting glance. 'While he's free,' he explained, 'he can lead us to whoever's behind the North Town opposition.' He started to turn away, then stopped as something else occurred to him. Turning back to Setright, he said with no little devilment, 'By the way, Fry's office is in a hell of a state. Be obliged if you'd run a mop across the floor before he rides in tomorrow morning.'

Setright's eyes rounded up and his cheeks went very red. 'What the deuce–?' he began.

But by that time Chase had already started off along the street, following the route Dexter had taken, and Jonah was falling into step beside him, a low chuckle bubbling in his throat.

The townsfolk who'd witnessed Dexter's downfall had congregated in shocked little clusters beneath the regularly-spaced municipal streetlamps to discuss what they'd seen. As they watched Chase and Jonah striding after him along the boardwalk, a new kind of hush enveloped the street, something more tense, more expectant and apprehensive. People scattered briskly to make way for them, and Jonah tickled the brim of his hat in acknowledgement as they went by, which only confused them more.

Throwing a glance at his companion, the black man said, 'You bearin' up, brother? You' lookin' a mite peaked.'

Chase was feeling peaked, too, but all he said was, 'I'm fine.'

They turned the corner and quickly sidestepped into the shadows of a porch overhang when they spotted Dexter no more than a hundred feet ahead of them, crossing the street diagonally in order to reach the far boardwalk. Jonah said in a quiet voice, 'You really think that Dexter feller's goan lead us to the big noise here'bouts?'

'Well, it's been known.'

They let Dexter stagger on for an additional fifty feet, then broke cover and continued after him. He kept stumbling along the sidestreet, looking neither right nor left, apparently intent on reaching his destination ... wherever in hell that turned out to be. As Chase had expected, he was heading in the direction of North Town. But when he'd gone about halfway down the street, he suddenly drew up outside a narrow, darkened, glass-fronted office building and started hammering on the door – and that wasn't what he'd been expecting at all.

Again the Spurlock men quickly sought a handy pool of shadow from which to spy on the beaten marshal. It was provided by the entrance to a slim little dog-trot almost directly opposite the building.

Dexter hammered some more, and a moment later Chase and Jonah spotted an oval of light inside the premises that moved hurriedly towards the door. Chase squinted, trying to see who was carrying the lantern at shoulder-height, but the distance was too great and the light was too poor.

At last the door opened and Dexter, still cradling his hand, started jabbering away before another male voice quickly told him to be quiet and come inside. The door closed behind them, the oval of light moved back from whence it came, and darkness once again claimed the narrow building.

Chase looked at the inscription painted on the building's glass front. It matched the inscription that hung from a shingle above the door.

FELIX VAN OUTEN
Real Estate Insurance Loan Agent

'What do you make of *that?*' asked Jonah.

Chase shook his head. 'Could be something. Could be nothing. Either way, Setright might know. We'll ask him in the morning.'

He felt Jonah's flake-gold eyes bore into him. 'What's wrong with tonight?'

Chase straightened up from the half-crouch into which he had instinctively fallen and stepped out of the shadows. 'Because right now,' he replied, 'you and me're gonna take a look around North Town while we still got the chance.'

Jonah's frown only deepened. 'What the hell does that mean?'

Patiently Chase told him, 'It means that the next time we risk going down there, the word'll have gone out about us, about whose side we're on … and if I'm any judge of human nature, you can bet that some damn' fool 'll try to shoot us on sight. Maybe even Dexter himself.'

SIX

Tom Fry rode back into town at sun-up next morning, a heavy-set, stoop-shouldered man in his late forties who'd hardly slept a wink the night before and now looked and felt as jumpy as hell.

All the way out from the old Mills place, he'd been wondering what it would be like, coming back to Willow Bend after so long away. By the time he finally reined down in front of the marshal's office, his stomach was churning with a mixture of emotions, and he paused a while in the saddle, just to look at the building, and think, and remember.

There'd been times when he never thought he'd see this place again. Even now, just being back here in town was enough to make his guts clench reflexively.

But even as he thought about turning his

horse around and riding right back out of town, he dismissed the notion. He'd quit once, and the humiliation of it had almost torn him apart. So there'd be no more of that.

He dismounted and tethered his chestnut to the rack out front. Then, hitching at his gunbelt to get the hang of his Peacemaker more comfortable, he drew in a deep breath, squared his shoulders, climbed the three familiar, crumbling stone steps to the door and let himself inside.

He saw immediately that Setright was already in there waiting for him, as were Chase and Jonah. All three heads turned as he hesitated uncomfortably in the doorframe, and then Setright took his dead clay pipe from his mouth and, using a low, understanding voice that the Spurlock men hadn't heard before, said 'Morning, Tom. Welcome back.'

Fry came inside, closed the door behind him and mumbled a brief, self-conscious greeting of his own. He took off his high-crowned grey hat and made to toss it onto the coat-rack … until he realized that the coat-rack wasn't there any more.

Setright crossed the room and clapped the marshal on the back, then produced a copy of the latest edition of the *Advocate* from his jacket pocket. 'Well,' he said proudly, holding it out for Fry to see, 'what do you think?'

Fry's sad grey eyes traced the headline. It read:

TOWN WELCOMES BACK MARSHAL FRY!
Veteran Peace Officer Returns to
Willow Bend
As Predecessor Leaves Amid
Allegations of Corruption

'You're going to make a lot of people happy, coming back like this,' Setright predicted.

'And a lot of other people *mad*,' Fry added bleakly, taking the enamel coffee-cup Jonah fetched over and nodding his thanks.

'Specially Phil Dexter.'

Behind his wire-framed spectacles, the newspaperman regarded the marshal with a frown. 'You're not having second thoughts, are you, Tom?'

Fry made a quick, impatient gesture with the mug and said wretchedly, 'Aw, I don't know *what* I'm having. I can't hardly think straight for...' He struggled for the right words, said finally, 'It's just ... me comin' back like this ... what if the North Towners was to go after Phoebe again, to teach me a lesson? Bert told me you thought you heard a rider out there last night.'

Chase looked into Fry's seamed, nut-brown face, at the tight pinch of the lips beneath his dusty black longhorn moustache. The man was worried sick, no good to himself or anyone else whilst his mind was elsewhere.

'Mebbe you'd feel a mite easier iffen someone wuz t'go back out there and ride shotgun on yo' wife until this thing's over,' suggested Jonah.

Fry glanced at him. 'One of you fellers?' he asked hopefully. 'I mean, would you *mind?*'

Jonah threw a quick glance at Chase, who nodded assent. 'Be proud to,' he replied a moment later. 'Ah'll ride on out there directly, iffen you like. Ah recall the way.'

The marshal seemed to shed years as he hustled around the desk. 'I guess I'd better write you a note of introduction,' he said, lowering himself into the chair so that he could hunt up a legal pad. 'Just to set the wife's mind at rest.'

'You're a regular pair of Good Samaritans, aren't you?' Setright noted sarcastically. Then, addressing Fry, he said disdainfully, 'Just before you arrived, Donovan was saying that we ought to arrange a meeting with the North Towners.'

'A *Public* meeting,' Chase corrected. 'A chance to let them hear your side of the argument, for you to tell 'em what they stand to gain by supporting your ordinances – and a chance for them to have *their* say, too.'

Setright chuckled grimly. 'Doesn't that sound cosy? The only trouble is, the North Towners made their minds up to oppose us long ago, and no amount of debate will change that.'

'How'd you *know* that, Mr Setright?' asked Jonah. 'When wuz the las' time you went down to North Town, anyways?'

Setright said piously, 'I don't make it my business to go there at *all*, if I can help it.'

'Well, mebbe you should. Me an' Chase, we went down there las' night, right after that little donnybrook with Dexter. You talk to them folks down there, an' Ah think you'll find you ain't got near as much opposition as you reckon.'

'Nonsense!'

'It's true,' said Chase. 'We did the rounds for more'n an hour, just to get the feel of the place. Most of the bartenders, gamblers and whores we spoke to had no real objections to your ordinances. They seemed to think they'd make up the cost of the licences quickly enough. Same with your liquor tax.'

'But we've had no end of trouble with them—'

'You've had no end of trouble with a small, hard *core* of them,' Chase amended. 'But as far as we could see, you've got no quarrel with the majority.'

Fry cleared his throat. 'I don't understand. If they're all so happy with what we're proposing, why should anyone want to cause us so much grief?'

Jonah shrugged. 'Mebbe they's just ornery. Or then again, mebbe whoever's behind all the rough stuff's got more to lose than the rest.'

'Can you think of anyone who'd fit that bill?' asked Chase.

Setright and Fry both pondered the question for a while, but came up empty. 'No-one,' the marshal replied after a moment.

'What about Felix Van Outen?'

The name, coming right out of the blue, surprised both townsmen. Setright said, 'You mean the realtor on First Street? What

141

the dickens does *he* have to do with North Town?'

'We tailed Dexter last night,' Chase explained. 'We were hoping he'd lead us to whoever's been organizing the North Towners against you, but instead he led us to this man Van Outen. Now, why do you suppose that was?'

Fry ran splayed fingers up through his collar-length, peppery black hair. 'Beats me. He's just a businessman. Came over from some place in Europe 'bout ten years ago, Holland, I think, and settled here in Willow Bend. But as far as I'm aware, his dealings've always been legal and above-board.' He fell silent a moment, then hazarded, 'Maybe Dexter wasn't thinking straight. Ernie said you didn't exactly spare his feelin's none. Maybe he went there... I don't know. For advice, maybe. Van Outen's a pretty clever feller. Could be Dexter wanted to find out exactly where he stood, in the eyes of the law.'

'Sounds pretty weak to me,' Chase murmured thoughtfully. 'No, he went straight to Van Outen for a purpose. Maybe I ought to sashay along to that realtor's office and ask him why.'

'You just hold that thought right where it is,' Setright cut in. 'It's just as Tom says. Felix Van Outen is a respectable member of this community, and neither you nor anyone else will go casting aspersions on his integrity.'

'Don't tell me,' Chase said without appreciable humour. 'He's a regular advertiser in your newspaper.'

Setright's lips bunched up around his dead pipe. 'That's got nothing to do with it,' he breathed.

'Well, someone down in North Town's stirring up all kinds of ill-feeling against you, and I'm not even sure if *they* know who it is.'

Setright moved over to the window beside the door and peered out at the slowly-wakening town. Chase looked down at Fry who, having found a stub of pencil at last, was quickly constructing a note to his wife. 'What do *you* reckon, marshal?' he asked.

Fry looked up, sparing Setright only the briefest glance. 'I think you're wasting your time if you think Van Outen's this kingpin you're after,' he replied after a moment. 'But I don't recall any law that says a man can't ask a few questions. Just make sure you do it polite, and don't go casting any of them things John just said about.'

Checking the wall-clock to make sure he wouldn't be too early, Chase touched the brim of his Montana peak and headed for the door. 'Looks like I'll be seeing you gents later, then.'

'You won't be seein' me, brother,' said Jonah. 'Ah'll be ridin' shotgun on Mrs Fry.'

Chase nodded, remembering. 'Well, you watch yourself, *amigo*,' he replied, and was surprised to find that he really *meant* it.

'By the way,' said Fry. 'I like the idea of a meetin'. Reckon we'll do what we can to organize one.'

Over by the window, Setright did some more muttering.

Ernie Weems finished sweeping down the boardwalk in front of his store and then narrowed his pleasant hazel eyes critically at the pure, powder blue sky beyond the porch overhang. It was going to be another glorious day, and that pleased him no end, because glorious days were good for trade.

Humming softly to himself, he turned and went back into the store, which was a good-size building in a prime position, with three counters flanking a central, black pot-belly stove, and stock-filled shelves rising from floor to ceiling behind each one.

He went around behind the farthest counter and stood his broom in the corner. Early morning was his favourite time of day, a quiet, reflective period when he was able to catch up on the inventory or the accounts, or just remind himself of how proud his parents would be if they could see him now. But this was no time for idling. There were still chores to do.

He brushed down the front of his white apron and checked by feel the knot of the string tie beneath his celluloid collar, then quickly smoothed his short, oiled brown hair flat with the palms of his hands.

He crossed the store to a keg of apples, hefted it to his narrow chest and carried it out onto the boardwalk. Next would come the keg of oranges all the way from California, and then a sack filled with sweet potatoes and finally one more keg stacked with crackers. It was hard work, but he enjoyed it.

Just as he was setting the last keg down, a loose board behind him creaked gently and a shadow fell across the keg of apples he'd just set down. Coming out of his reverie, he turned and began to rise, smiling as he did so. 'Morning–'

The greeting died on his lips.

A massive Negro was towering over him. The man stood easily six and a half feet in height, with broad, sloping shoulders from which hung long, muscular arms and big hands with scarred knuckles. The torso was muscular too, almost too wide to accommodate the man's elegant black frock coat and brocade vest, but it narrowed to a trim waist and a flat belly, and the legs below it extended long, solid and powerful to a surprisingly small pair of feet, clad now in Hessian ankle-boots.

The man's name was Quintus Ashe, and he owned two saloons in North Town.

Weems straightened carefully out of his crouch, keeping his movements slow and easy for fear of antagonizing the stocky, muscular, golden pit bull that was Ashe's constant companion. Even so, the dog's dark, spittle-shiny lips peeled back to show a serrated line of ivory-white teeth, and its growl came deep and menacing up out of its deep chest to fill the early morning air.

Quintus Ashe said, 'Quiet, Jack,' and Jack, the pit bull, stopped growling, but didn't take his baleful, unblinking black glare off Weems' pale, frightened face.

'Morning, Mr Ashe,' the storekeeper said at last.

Ashe lifted a long, polished cane with a

solid silver knob-handle to the broad brim of his white planter's hat. He looked as elegant as the storekeeper had ever seen him, and smelled strongly of pomatum. 'Mr Weems,' he replied.

When he said no more, Weems asked, 'Is there, ah … something I can get you?'

'Some gumdrops for Jack,' Ashe replied in his quiet, vaguely menacing way. 'He has a sweet tooth, that one. Several, in fact.'

'Uh, sure.'

Weems turned and hustled back into the store, all too aware of Ashe's long, rhythmic stride behind him, and the eager skittering of the dog's stocky legs and the scratch and scrape of its long claws against the board floor. Uncomfortably he wondered why Ashe had come into the store this morning. He'd never called in before. They knew each other by sight and reputation, and that was all – though Ashe's reputation was a terrible, violent, unpredictable one.

As if having read his thoughts, the Negro said conversationally, 'I understand there was some trouble last night.'

'Trouble?'

'A fight between Marshal Dexter and … another man.'

'Oh. Yes. I heard … something about it.'

'*What* did you hear?'

'Oh, you know,' hedged Weems, finishing lamely, 'Idle gossip.'

He went behind the counter and fished the gumdrop jar out from beneath a pilfer-proof glass dome. 'How, ah … how many?' he asked nervously.

Ashe inclined his huge shoulders. He was about forty, with a face that was long and mournful, cheekbones pronounced, jawline firm and very definite. His eyes were dark, inscrutable, the whites shot through with blood, the nose broad, broken at least once but fixed by an expert, the thick lips a peculiar plum colour. A small tracery of scars criss-crossed Ashe's eyes, and his ears were cauliflowered ever so slightly. 'Let's not be mean,' he replied. 'Give me a dollar's-worth.'

'A dollar's-worth it is,' Weems replied, hoping that Ashe wouldn't notice the tremble of his hands as he weighed out the required amount.

As he poured the gumdrops into a bag, the black man fished out a dollar and flipped it onto the counter, asking idly, 'Who is he, this man who takes the law into his own hands?'

Weems gestured ignorance. 'Beats me.' He slipped the dollar into the drawer till.

'And yet, as I understand it,' said Ashe, 'you were seen in his company just hours before he attacked Marshal Dexter.'

Startled by the comment, Weems looked up into the other man's bloodshot eyes. He found no hint of menace there. Ashe just looked curious. And yet the storekeeper still felt threatened, compelled to tell the truth or face truly dire consequences.

He tried to decide what to say. He'd never liked Ashe. The man was cold, imperious, accustomed to getting his own way. For all Weems knew, he was the force behind the

North Town bullies. If that were the case, could he *really* tell a potential enemy everything he knew? He swallowed noticeably, thought, *No, No, I can't do that.*

'There must be some mistake–' he began.

Ashe smiled indulgently, with his lips alone, and said, 'Jack?'

At its master's command, the pit bull ran around in a tight circle, searching out just the right spot, then sniffed at the pot-bellied stove for a few moments before raising one hind leg and relieving himself.

Weems watched the dark puddle spread across the freshly-swept floor and swallowed again. Blood rushed to his cheeks, and his breathing quickened to a rasping, painful saw. 'Please, Mr Ashe! There … there's no call for that kind of behaviour. That dog–'

'*Jack,* you mean?' said Ashe, and at its name the pit bull padded back over, paused beside its master and started growling ominously. 'Let me tell you something about Jack, Mr Weems,' Ashe said quietly. 'Imagine if you will that he is not so much a *dog* as a gladiator of old, a creature bred to fight, to kill and to *die,* if need be, for the entertainment of his master and his audience. Imagine that, Mr Weems, and you will begin to truly appreciate what manner of creature you see before you.'

Warming to his subject, Ashe continued in the same quiet tone. 'This ... gladiator ... of ours, is a marvel of nature, the product of many years' careful, selective breeding, breeding which has given him speed and determination, courage and strength. Jack is not just a *dog,* Mr Weems. He is fifty pounds of pure *killer.* And if I tell him to attack, he will do so without hesitation. Man or beast, it makes little difference to Jack. He will do my bidding and nothing short of a bullet will stop him.'

Somehow Weems tore his eyes away from the panting dog. 'Are ... are you threatening me?' he croaked around the lump in his throat.

Ashe frowned disapproval at the suggestion. 'Not threatening, Mr Weems. Merely advising you as to what could happen if Jack got the wrong impression and decided that you were *lying* to me.'

Weems swallowed some more, his eyes shuttling back and forth between Ashe and the dog. All at once the store seemed airless, too small. He felt a bead of sweat worm down the side of his face but stifled the impulse to reach up and wipe it away in case the dog mistook his intention and reacted accordingly.

'I'm waiting,' Ashe said in a voice that was quietly, confidently mocking.

Somehow Weems found the courage to say, 'If I knew anything, I'd t-tell you...'

Ashe shook his head. 'I think we had better start again, Mr Weems. And I warn you. There's no stopping Jack once he gets started. The animal is fearless, afraid of no man and no *thing*...'

It was at just that moment that the dog happened to look behind him, and suddenly its ears flattened to its broad, squarish head and its thin tail notched lower and lower until it was tucked between the animal's slightly bowed back legs.

With an apologetic glance at its owner, Jack stopped growling and slunk to the far corner.

For the first time that Ernie Weems could remember, something other than supreme confidence showed on Quintus Ashe's face. He registered surprise at the dog's reaction, then turned to see what had caused such a marked change in the animal's demeanour.

He saw a tall man with hawkish features and cool green eyes standing in the doorway. The man was looking at the dog, *smiling* at him.

Weems's eyelids fluttered with relief. *Donovan!* He hadn't thought it possible to be so happy to see anyone. Then Chase came deeper into the store and Weems heard him remark, 'Skittish kinda dog you got there, mister.'

If the newcomer was at all daunted by Ashe's great size, it didn't show. Chase merely treated the man to the same kind of smile he'd bestowed upon the dog, either unaware of the aura of menace that clung to Ashe, or unimpressed by it.

'Skittish?' Ashe rumbled. 'I can assure you, sir, that Jack is afraid of no man.'

Chase only shrugged.

Recovering himself, Ashe said, 'Quintus Ashe is the name, stranger. And you'd be…?'

Chase held up an apple. 'I'd be coming in to buy some breakfast,' he replied innocently.

Ashe narrowed his eyes, used his fancy cane to indicate Chase's face. 'It appears that you are something of a pugilist,' he said. 'I used to be a prize-fighter myself.'

'Well,' said Chase, 'I sure hope you always won your fights, mister. *I* do.'

Ashe studied him a moment longer. Then, realizing that this green-eyed newcomer wasn't about to disappear, he turned back to Weems. 'Good-day, Mr Weems,' he said in his very courteous, deliberate fashion. 'I'll be seeing you again. *Jack!*'

The dog fairly scooted from the store,

relieved to put some distance between it and the man who kept smiling at it. Ashe, by contrast, picked up his purchase and quit the building at a slower pace, and when he was gone, some of the tension in the air left with him.

Chase held out the apple. 'How much do I owe you?'

Weems shook his head distractedly. 'On the house.'

Chase took a bite. 'Well, well,' he mused. 'What the hell did *he* want?'

Weems told him, finishing shakily, 'Oh Lord, I was so glad when you stepped through the door–' He stopped suddenly, then asked, 'Did you really come in just to buy an apple?'

Chase shook his head, still trying to puzzle out where Ashe fitted into this business. One thing was certain, however. He'd stirred the North Towners up, all right, made them curious. He headed for the door, still eating the apple.

'Uh, Mr Donovan?'

Weems looked a little sheepish when Chase turned back to him. 'Yeah?'

'I was just... I mean...' He took a deep breath. 'What should I do ... you know, if Ashe, ah ... if he comes back?'

Chase threw a quick look around the store. 'You sell guns, don't you?' he replied. 'Load one.'

In daylight, Van Outen's office looked as un-remarkable as it had the previous night, just a plain wooden structure with a dusty plate-glass frontage that was squeezed between two equally unremarkable stores.

Chase reached his destination five minutes later, twisted the handle without breaking stride, shoved the door open and followed it into a small, dark office that was cluttered with file cabinets and three low shelves stacked with dusty-looking books and ledgers. A frail-looking little picket fence cut the room in two, and set into the back wall beyond it stood a pebbled-glass door that presumably marked the position of Van

Outen's inner sanctum.

A girl with shining auburn hair worn in a loose, attractive shower of curls was standing behind a desk just inside the doorway with her back to him. She turned at the sound of the bell suspended from the frame, and he saw that she'd been busy watering a collection of sketchy plants on a scarred wall-shelf.

She smiled a pleasant, open smile that made her cheeks dimple appealingly, and set down her dainty little watering-can before she said brightly, 'Good morning. Can I help you?'

Chase figured her to be in her early twenties. She stood at least a foot shorter than he, and beneath her sober, neck-to-ankle lavender and white-lace dress, her body looked full and generous.

'Van Outen,' he replied. 'Is he in?'

'Might I ask the nature of your business, Mr...?'

'Donovan,' he told her. 'And it's private.'

He saw the warmth go out of her wide,

well-spaced blue eyes, and realized that his cold, direct attitude had killed the good mood she'd been in. She gave a brisk nod, accepting that he was not a man for polite small talk, and said more formally, 'I'll see if Mr Van Outen can spare you a few moments.'

For the first time that he could recall, he actually regretted his behaviour, and to make amends, he gestured to the plants before she could step around the desk and head for the far end of the room. 'You, ah, seem to have a way with plants, ma'am,' he said hurriedly. 'They look real...' he searched for the word, didn't find it and finished lamely, '...well, *green*, I guess.'

It was such a dumb thing to say that she giggled before she could stop herself, and that brought a very fetching blush to her otherwise pale, fresh skin. As the ice in her eyes thawed, she said, 'I do my best. Plants and flowers do cheer the place up so, don't you think?'

He nodded. 'I do indeed, ma'am,' he

replied, lying through his teeth.

She let herself through the little picket fence and rapped on the door at the far end of the room. When a muffled voice called out, 'Come!' she went inside and closed the door behind her.

Left alone, Chase shook his head. What in hell was happening to him? What did he care if he spoiled the girl's humour? He was here to do a job that could get him or Jonah killed if it wasn't handled right. It wasn't a popularity contest, there wasn't any time to consider a person's *feelings!* In any case, if the girl was somehow involved in this affair, she'd get more than her feelings hurt before it was over.

Just then she came back outside and called, 'Mr Van Outen will see you now.'

He nodded thanks and went through the door, which she closed behind him. The office in which he found himself was smaller than that occupied by the girl, and scrupulously tidy. A man was standing behind a desk in the far corner, his right hand extended in welcome. Behind him sat a big grey Jenks & Millbush safe.

'Mr Donovan, is it?' asked Felix Van Outen.

He wasn't at all what Chase had been expecting. He was tall, and looked skinnier than a rake in his sober black suit and modest grey cravat. He was about sixty, bald, but with a close-cropped white fuzz of hair above his jug-handle ears. His large head was balanced on a scrawny neck in which danced an over-active Adam's apple.

He looked just like everyone's favourite granpaw.

Ignoring the proffered hand, Chase said, 'Like to ask you a couple questions, if that's all right.'

'Of course, of course,' said Van Outen, apparently taking no offence at his visitor's refusal to shake, instead using the extended hand to indicate the chair on the other side of the desk. 'How can I help you?'

'You can tell me what Phil Dexter was doing here late last night.'

Seating himself, Van Outen allowed his kindly blue eyes to mirror puzzlement. 'The *marshal,* you mean?' he asked. He rubbed a jaw to which clung the faintest white stubble, missed during that morning's ablutions. His hands were skeletal, with long, very clean fingers.

'Not any more,' said Chase.

'You are here in an *official* capacity?' the realtor asked curiously. 'You *too* are an officer of the law?' His English was very good, although he spoke it with a strong accent, pronouncing every 's' sound more like a 'sh'.

Chase shrugged noncommittally, knowing he'd get nothing out of the man if he told him the truth. 'I watched him banging at your door last night, saw you let him in. I'd like to know why that was.'

Van Outen shook his head, and the movement made his yellowish jowls quiver. 'That I cannot say. There is a certain degree of ... confidentiality ... between a man in my position and his clients. However, I will tell you this much. Marshal Dexter was extremely … distressed, when he showed up here. He came to seek my opinion on the … validity … of your actions last evening, and that is precisely what I gave him. Is that not good enough?'

'Not hardly. If Dexter wanted advice, he'd have been better off going to see a lawyer. Why'd he come to you?'

'We have had … dealings, in the past. A loan was made, the debt repaid with interest. I have advised him many times on one matter or another. I would not go so far as to say that a friendship exists between us, but certainly I think he trusts my judgements in … various matters.'

'You have any business dealings with North Town, Mr Van Outen?'

Finally losing his patience, the Dutchman snapped, 'I don't see what any of this has got to do with me. I am a simple, hard-working businessman, as anyone in this town will tell you. A God-fearing man, Mr Donovan, who goes to church every Sunday. Can you say as much about yourself?'

Chase got up. 'All right, no need to get your bowels in an uproar. Just one more question and then I'm out of here.'

Van Outen said stiffly, 'If you must.'

'Is Quintus Ashe another of your clients?'

The realtor didn't even bat an eyelid. 'Who is Quintus Ashe?' he asked. 'And just who are *you?* You ask me all these questions, but you don't even show me any identification.'

Chase sighed and headed for the door. 'Forget it,' he replied. 'Sorry to've troubled you.'

Van Outen watched him leave, his expression a mixture of indignation and injured pride as he fidgeted with his collar and cravat, and brushed at the lapels of his jacket with trembling hands.

Chase closed the door behind him and stood for a moment, pondering his next step. It looked as if Marshal Fry had been right about Van Outen. Questioning the man had been a complete waste of time. So where did that leave him?

It left him still wondering where Quintus Ashe fitted into it.

'Is everything all right, Mr Donovan?'

Looking around, Chase saw that the girl, Van Outen's secretary, had come back down from the front of the building and was regarding him with concern.

He nodded. 'Fine, Miss…?'

'MacNair,' she replied, offering him her hand. 'Emily MacNair.'

He took the hand. Just as he expected, it felt cool and soft. With a rare smile he touched the brim of his hat and went past her, out onto the street.

At once his mind returned to Quintus Ashe. According to Weems, Ashe owned two saloons in North Town. But that alone wouldn't give him enough reason to stir up so much trouble about the new ordinances. Unless…

Unless Ashe had more business interests in North Town than he was letting on.

There was one sure way to find out, and that was to check the records and see who *really* owned what down there. His mouth thinned with distaste at the prospect because, like all men of action, he hated paperwork with a vengeance. But it just had to be done.

He toyed fleetingly with the idea of going back into Van Outen's place and asking Emily MacNair where they stored such records in Willow Bend, but quickly changed his mind. He felt reasonably certain that neither she nor Van Outen were involved with the North Towners, but you never knew.

In any case, Weems would know. He'd go back and ask him … and he'd grab himself another couple of apples whilst he was about it.

SEVEN

Left alone in his office after John Setright and Jonah Kissing said their goodbyes, Tom Fry sat at his old desk and debated what to do next.

By rights he guessed he should take a turn around town, let himself be seen and make sure that everything out there was nice and peaceful. He certainly felt easier in his mind knowing that Kissing would be keeping an eye on Phoebe, and he figured he could use the exercise. But he wasn't sure he could face going out there, and maybe risk making himself a target, just yet.

Face it, Tom, he told himself angrily. *The bastards shot your nerve to hell, and it's gonna take you a helluva time to get it back. That's if you ever do.*

Feeling restless and wretched, he rose

167

from behind the desk, went over to the stove and started pouring himself another cup of coffee he didn't really want. He threw the pot down with an irritable curse, snatched up his hat and strode across to the door, but faltered before reaching for the handle.

No... He wasn't ready for that yet.

He cast the hat aside and wandered around the room, wondering if he'd done the right thing, coming back to Willow Bend. Wouldn't it have been better to wait until Phoebe felt more like travelling and then just start up again someplace else? Wouldn't that have been wiser, safer? Sure it would. But he was too old to be starting life anew, and so was the missus. They knew this town, its people. They had friends here–

The sound of the door clicking open made him turn – and freeze. Because Phil Dexter was standing in the doorway.

For a long, heavy moment they just stared at each other. Dexter looked like hell. His square jaw was swollen and so was his nose. There were little cuts in the lips beneath his white-blond steerhorn moustache and his left hand was tied with a bandage. He glared sullenly at Fry from beneath lowered brows, until Fry opened his mouth and said cautiously, 'What brings you here, Phil?'

Dexter glanced around, his gaze finally lingering on a small bundle which had been thrown carelessly into one corner, and upon which had been coiled a double-hung gunbelt and matching Colts. 'Came for my things,' he growled.

'Well, get 'em and then haul freight.'

Dexter crossed the room, moving carefully because his ribs and muscles were still protesting from his encounter with Chase the previous night. Fry watched him bend and hook up the gunbelt, a sick feeling in his guts.

'You know something, Tom?' said Dexter. 'I'm disappointed in you. Always had you down as a man who'd fight his own battles, not hire a gun to do it for him. Guess I was wrong, huh?'

'You weren't wrong, Phil.'

'Then who the hell's Donovan?'

A memory suddenly occurred to Fry, and his lips twitched briefly. 'Just a Good Samaritan,' he replied.

'What the hell does that mean?'

'You wouldn't understand.'

Awkwardly, still favouring his bandaged hand, Dexter strapped his gunbelt around his lean waist, then scooped the small bundle up in his wounded hand and headed for the door. He stopped before he reached it though, and slowly turned back to face the marshal. He stood with his legs slightly parted, and his good right hand hanging within reach of the .38 that was holstered on that hip. 'You're a fool, Tom,' he said. 'You could've gone far away from here and lived to see old age. You *and* Phoebe. But you just threw it all away.'

Later, Fry realized that it was hearing Phoebe's name that worked some kind of weird, healing magic inside him. He looked closer at Dexter and expected to feel fear but didn't. Instead, for the first time, he saw what a self-serving sonofabitch Dexter really was, and somehow that gave the marshal an ability to see himself in a kinder light, to feel an assurance that, although his nerve *had* snapped, it could and *would* be fixed.

He heard himself say, 'Any time you want to try your luck, Phil, you go right ahead.'

Not expecting that, Dexter's fathomless brown eyes widened momentarily, until his battered face flattened out again. 'I'm gonna burn you down, Tom,' he said quietly.

'You're gonna *try*,' Fry corrected with sudden, unnerving confidence. 'There's a difference.'

Dexter's fingers flexed slowly, threateningly, like the legs of some fat, flesh-coloured spider. He said, 'Bold talk for an old man who ran out when the going got rough.'

'Look at me,' Fry countered. 'I'm not running *now*.'

Silence congealed in the wood-panelled room. Fry said roughly, 'If you're gonna haul iron, do it and quit stinkin' up my office, you woman-beatin' sonofabitch.'

Dexter's split lips compressed angrily, and his fingers started flexing faster, but still he didn't go for the .38.

'*Well?*' demanded Fry.

He could see that Dexter was trying to screw up enough courage to make his play. Muscles tightened around his mouth, and his eyes narrowed. The flexing fingers worked faster, faster … but *still* he didn't do anything about it.

Losing patience with him, Fry said disdainfully, 'Ah, get out of my sight, Phil. I see you on the streets of this town again, I'll kill you, and the law be damned.'

He thought that would finally push Dexter into making his move. But even as he watched, the killing light went out of Dexter's eyes. The man swore beneath his breath, because this wasn't the Fry he'd been expecting to find, then screwed around and wrenched the door open.

He stamped out and Fry crossed the waxed floorboards to watch him go down the steps and tear the reins of his waiting horse from the rack. Dexter grabbed his saddlehorn and dragged himself across leather, then turned the animal in a tight circle and galloped north without a backward glance.

Fry leaned against the doorframe and watched him go. The day was warming up now, and the strong morning sunshine gave Main Street a clean look. For just this moment, Willow Bend was a town without shadows. *His* town.

Damn, it felt good.

All at once he felt more like taking a turn around town after all, and was just about to go back inside and fetch his hat when he noticed three riders walking their dusty, ill-used horses in from the south.

He watched them come nearer. They kept their mounts to the middle of the street, and they slumped in their hulls like men who'd travelled a fair piece.

As he ran his eyes across them, Fry's mood soured. He looked from one newcomer to the next, saw a clean-shaven man with spiteful blue eyes and pocked skin, another with a crimson bandanna at his throat, bearded and with a drinker's nose, and the third, also bearded, with a round, lined face that was deeply tanned. This feller wore his gun in a black leather holster that was decorated with silver studs.

He knew better than to judge a man on first impressions, but he'd packed a badge long enough to recognize trouble when he saw it.

The trio passed the law office with nary a sideways glance. Fry watched them go, wondering who they were and what had brought them to town.

For the sake of his fractured nerves, he was better off not knowing.

By the end of the afternoon, several large posters had sprung up all over town, courtesy of a sceptical John Setright. They read:

MEETING!
TO BE HELD AT THE

MUNICIPAL HALL
7 O'CLOCK
TOMORROW NIGHT!
TO DISCUSS
THE PROPOSED ORDINANCES
LISTED BELOW
ALL WELCOME!

In a plush office above one of his two saloons, Quintus Ashe turned away from the lace-bedecked window, threw another gumdrop high and watched his pet dog snap it effortlessly out of the air.

The smallest of smiles pulled at his plum-coloured lips as he bent to scrub fondly at the tight golden fur that crowned the pit bull's large, flat head. Outside, dusk was falling across the maze of narrow streets that made up North Town, dyeing the purple sky with amber streamers. Small, dusty windows were filling with smoky yellow lamplight, and judging by the sounds floating up to him from below, the evening's business was already getting underway.

'Go on,' he said, addressing a man standing on the other side of the expensively-furnished room.

The man, Cotton Jones, had worked as Ashe's head barkeep for more than three years. Tall but paunchy, bald but for a crown of thick hair that was as black as jet, Cotton wore a small broom of a moustache beneath his big, pitted nose. Shrugging the broad shoulders beneath his collarless, striped cotton shirt, he replied, 'Well, that's about all there is to it. These three fellers came in late this afternoon, ordered whiskey and, well, you know what it's like, they jus' got to talkin'. Askin', really.'

'About Donovan,' said Ashe.

Cotton nodded. 'Couldn't believe my luck when they jus' walked right in off the street an' told me everythin' I wanted to hear. I mean, you'd only jus' told me to keep my ears open, right?'

Another gumdrop sailed through the air, and the pit bull's hungry jaws closed with a tight, audible snap, swallowing it whole.

''Course, I didn't give nothin' away, just played it real close, ast 'em who he was, this feller they was lookin' for,' Cotton continued. 'One of 'em, tall feller with bad skin and a little scar under one eye, said his name was Al Devlin, he tells me Donovan used to be a Ranger, killed his brother.' He leaned forward, and the light from the ornate chandelier directly above him reflected in his very smooth pate. *Used* to be,' he repeated meaningfully. 'He says they kicked him outta the Battalion 'cause he was too damn' keen with his gun. Way this Devlin tells it, the Rangers were glad to be rid of him.'

'So he's no one official,' Ashe mused thoughtfully.

'Devlin says the las' time he saw him, Donovan was turning into a grade-one drunk,' Cotton confirmed. 'Anyway, turns out that someone spotted Donovan comin' up this way from Del Rio. Devlin got word of it an' come lookin' for him, but lost his trail somewheres along the line.'

Ashe nodded and threw Jack another

gumdrop. 'They're looking to … *settle* … with Donovan, are they?'

'Devlin didn't make no secret of it.'

'Are they still downstairs?'

Cotton offered his boss a sly gin. 'Yeah. I told 'em I'd ask around, see if I could find Donovan for 'em, just to make sure they didn't go no place else until I'd had a word with you.'

'Good man.'

When Ashe said no more, Cotton hesitated uncertainly. 'What you want I should do now, then, Mr Ashe?' he asked after a moment.

Ashe considered the question with just a hint of wry amusement. Even after all this time, Cotton still didn't realize that he, Ashe, never made any of the really important decisions. That was always left to an older and possibly wiser head, someone he was always required to consult first. Idly he flipped Jack another gumdrop. 'Find out where they're staying. Tell them you might have a lead on Donovan's whereabouts and that you'll get word to them as soon as you turn anything up.'

Cotton nodded again. 'Gotcha,' he said, and left the room.

As soon as he was gone, Ashe crossed the floor and grabbed his jacket off the back of the button-studded leather chair behind his enormous desk. He shrugged into it, then clapped his broad-brimmed planter's hat back on his head and reached for his cane.

All the while, Jack followed his every movement with undivided attention, for he knew that where his master went, so did he. And just like his master, Jack was always ready to swagger through the streets of Willow Bend, scaring the crap out of everyone he passed.

'I thought I told you never to come here,' snapped Felix Van Outen.

The Dutchman had been in a foul mood ever since Chase had paid him a visit earlier in the day. He had cursed Dexter's stupidity in leading Donovan straight to him, and then he'd started wondering just who the man could be, and where he'd gotten hold of Quintus Ashe's name.

The realtor's natural impulse had been to remove the threat Donovan posed right away. But almost at once his orderly, businessman's mind had urged caution. He must find out exactly who his enemy was before he dared to act, for if Donovan proved to be a US Marshal, a Ranger or even a Pinkerton, then one single, rash move would bring him even more trouble than he had right now.

And talking of trouble, the last thing he needed at the moment was this clandestine visit from Ashe and his confounded dog, although to be fair, at least the big man had had sense enough to arrive by the back door.

Normally, Ashe never showed his face unless he was summoned. In public, and at Van Outen's insistence, the two men always kept their distance from each other, so that no one would ever dream that an association existed between them.

And it had worked well. Van Outen

schemed and planned, and Ashe and his minions carried out those plans, often ruthlessly and with extreme violence. It was a partnership out of which neither man fared badly, and which carried little risk...

Until Marshal Fry and his sanctimonious confederates had tried to clean up North Town, that was.

And until this man Donovan had turned up.

In the turned-low lamplight, Van Outen's eyes were a pale, icy blue, and the pupils were very small. He no longer looked like a benign grandfather, he looked like something incalculably more evil. He tapped the poster that was spread out across his desk and said, 'You've seen these, I take it? Setright fetched one in and asked me to display it. What could I do? I have to be seen to be doing my part.'

Ashe's dark, bloodshot eyes dropped to the bold lettering and he said in mild surprise, 'Surely you don't think this could *hurt* us? It's only a meeting. And the success of any meeting depends on how many people show up.'

The Dutchman regarded him with something approaching contempt. Ashe really couldn't see the dangers this meeting presented. If such an assembly were allowed to go ahead, and even a small proportion of North Towners attended, it could very well teach them that most basic rule of survival – that there was safety in numbers. If they learned that, it was only a matter of time before they also learned to resist. And then…

But how could he expect Ashe to appreciate that? Ashe was and always would be hired muscle, despite his predilection for the finer things in life, and his childish desire to be seen as something more than the bare-knuckle plantation fighter he'd been before he received his freedom from slavery and turned professional.

Van Outen sat down behind his desk and said, 'Well, you're here now. *Why?* And it had better be good.'

'It is,' said Ashe. And he told the Dutchman everything he had learned from Cotton Jones.

At the end of it, Van Outen smiled his first real smile of the day.

'You see what I'm saying,' said Ashe.

Of course Van Outen saw. This man Donovan had come here with no authority whatsoever. He had doubtless been hired by Fry and the other so-called 'concerned citizens'. Which meant that, if he were to meet an untimely end, who would give a damn? And what would anyone really *do* about it?

His death might also shock the townsfolk into abandoning their precious meeting tomorrow night.

Furthermore, no one could pin Donovan's death on anyone from North Town. The men who wanted him dead had come in from elsewhere to settle what was essentially a private score. Hell, he wouldn't even have to *pay* to get rid of Donovan!

The smile grew into a low, unsettling chuckle.

'Shall I arrange it?' asked Ashe, already

knowing the answer.

Van Outen nodded, suddenly feeling quite cheery. 'Yes,' he said. 'Send word to this man Devlin and his cronies. Tell them where they'll find Donovan tonight. And tell them that, if our gallant town marshal should try to intervene when the shooting starts, they can gun *him* down, too.'

Ashe smiled and touched his cane to the brim of his hat. 'I'm on my way,' he said, and headed for the back door with Jack scrabbling and panting at his heels.

Chase quit Willow Bend's municipal building just as afternoon started fading towards early evening. He'd spent most of the day sifting through the town's dusty, ill-kept records, a largely frustrating exercise which had done little to improve his already low opinion of paperwork. Now, with an aching back and sore eyes, he made his way slowly back to the law office.

Marshal Fry was just finishing some filing when he came through the door, and he watched Chase pull up a ladderback chair and flop tiredly into it before saying, 'Long day?'

'You *could* say that.'

'But did it *get* you anywhere?'

'Well, you were right about Van Outen,' he replied. 'I don't think he's involved. But I got to thinking about something Jonah said this morning. These damned ordinances of yours, they wouldn't really hit anyone hard ... unless you owned a number of businesses in North Town. Then you'd be paying out for one licence after another, not to mention all the extra cash you'd be turning over in liquor taxes.'

Fry squinted at him as he took his own seat. 'I see what you're gettin' at,' he said. 'But no one person owns that much property down there.'

'I know,' Chase replied tiredly. 'I checked. Most all the properties in North Town are owned by different people – until you check the names of those people against the names listed in your register of voters. That's when it starts to get real interesting.'

'How so?'

Chase countered the question with one of his own. 'You know a feller named Frank Willard, marshal? Or Sam Cooper? How 'bout John Goldman? Or Mike Hallaran?'

Fry gave it a moment's thought, then shook his head. 'Can't say as I do. *Should* I?'

'According to your land records, they all own and run properties in North Town ... but none of them show up on your register of voters. And they're not the only ones. I can quote you at least another dozen.'

Fry slowly eased back in his chair. The office was darkening as the day slowly died. 'The North Towners keep to themselves, Donovan. Maybe they just didn't bother to register. It's not obligatory, you know.'

'Maybe. But I'll bet you had a delegation from North Town on your doorstep when you first posted your ordinances, didn't you?'

'Uh-huh.'

'And I'll bet you knew just about every

man who turned up to protest.'

'I did.'

'But these fellers I just mentioned, you don't know their names and you've never seen 'em around town.' He shook his head. 'That's because they don't *exist,* marshal. They're just names, aliases, to protect the identity of the real owner.'

It went very quiet in the office while the marshal digested that. At last understanding dawned. 'So the man who has the most to lose is the man who's stirring up the rest of North Town,' he murmured thoughtfully. 'But who is he? How do we find out?'

Chase shrugged. 'I haven't worked that one out yet, but I'd be willing to lay generous odds that Quintus Ashe is involved in it somewhere.'

'Yeah, Ernie Weems mentioned that you two'd met each other. I'd be inclined to think that Ashe is involved myself, but without proof...' He reached up and scrubbed at his face. It had been a long day and he was tired, but ever since his encounter with Dexter, he'd also felt a sense of optimism that had been missing from his life for too long. He'd made a good start back in his old job, and this green-eyed, hawk-faced man who'd been sent to him by another man he would likely never meet, had made good progress towards solving the town's difficulties.

'You hungry?' he asked.

Chase said, 'Is a frog's ass watertight?'

Fry laughed and stood up. 'Come on, then. I'll stand you supper.'

An hour later, the two men said their good-nights on the boardwalk outside the café, and as Chase watched Fry head back to his office, he confessed to a strange sense of contentment. This job was presenting him with a challenge, something more than just riding after one owlhoot or another and bringing them back, alive if possible but more often dead. And though he was loath to admit it – even to himself – it wasn't so bad, letting other folks into your life, and making yourself a small part of theirs.

Jesus Christ, he told himself in disgust. *You*

must be getting soft between the ears.

Wincing, he straightened a little to ease his stiff back. It had been a long day and an early night sounded almighty tempting. Full dark had fallen by now and the street-traffic had thinned appreciably. In uncharacteristic good humour, he started ambling up towards the hotel ... unaware that his plans for a peaceful evening were just minutes away from exploding in a storm of blood and gunfire.

EIGHT

Before Chase could ask for his key, the desk clerk stammered, 'Ah, Mr Donovan. Thank goodness.'

He was in a high state of agitation, and quickly explained why. 'I caught a man in here no more than half an hour ago, looking through the register,' he said, adding, 'You know, as if he were trying to find … someone.'

Chase frowned at him. 'Me?'

The clerk's shrug said, *Who else?*

'What did he look like, this feller?'

'Mean,' the clerk remembered nervously. 'He had a kind of *mottled* skin, and a thin pink scar, right here.' He traced an imaginary three-inch line just below his left eye.

The description stirred a vague memory inside Chase, but the clerk could've been describing any one of a hundred men, so he didn't set much store by it. 'What did he have to say for himself?' he asked.

'Nothing,' the clerk replied. 'I was out back when I heard this noise, you see. I came out to see what it was and found him standing right where you're standing now, just … just checking through the register as bold as you please. When I asked him what he thought he was doing with hotel property, he just turned around and walked out. But he was up to no good, I swear it.'

He gave a delicate little shudder, then produced a small envelope upon which had been written Chase's name. 'And that's not all,' he added. 'Someone left this for you earlier on.'

Chase took it. 'Did you see who it was?'

'No, I'm sorry, I was—'

'—out back, yeah. Well, thanks anyway.'

He shoved both the letter and his key into a shirt pocket and headed for the stairs. The clerk called after him. 'What about the man, Mr Donovan?'

Chase shrugged. 'If wants me,' he replied, 'he knows where to find me.'

As he climbed the stairs, he decided it wouldn't do any harm to sleep light tonight, just in case the North Towners *were* planning something. In the meantime, who the hell was sending him—

His attention was suddenly taken by the distant nickering of a restless horse. He froze with one foot on the top step, his eyes travelling quickly to the window at the far end of the dingy hallway, which led out onto a set of fire stairs. The window had been opened just a fraction, and a pleasing breeze was stirring the thick lace curtain there.

Instinctively his right hand closed around the Vulcanite grips of his .44 and he eased the weapon gently in its oiled buscadero holster. Then he cat-footed down the hallway, dropping to a crouch and sweeping off his Montana peak when he reached the window. Slowly, carefully, he eased the curtain aside so that he could peer down into the dark alley that ran along the back and sides of the building.

A man was standing down below, facing away from him. The reins of three restive mounts were gathered together in his pudgy right fist. With his free hand, the man was stroking the muzzle of the most fidgety horse, trying to keep it quiet and calm. He wasn't having much luck.

Chase strained to identify the man, but there wasn't much to see in the poor light, just an impression of size – big – and a voluminous, bottle-green riding jacket. Even as he watched, however, the man turned his head a little and Chase got a brief, blurry look at his profile, saw a full, bearded face that was heavily-lined and deeply-tanned.

His lips formed a curse, because a lifetime ago he'd christened this man Silver Studs, after the fancy black-leather gunbelt he wore.

All at once he realized that the man with the mottled skin had been Grant Devlin's brother. Hell, no wonder he'd sounded vaguely familiar! And since Silver Studs was holding three horses, the chances were good that Devlin's other partner, another bearded man with shaggy eyebrows and a drinker's pitted nose, whom he'd christened Red Bandanna for his distinctive neckwear, was also around here someplace.

Someplace…

He thought about Devlin checking the register to find out what room he was staying in. He thought about the gallery that ran along the front of the building. He thought that any man who could climb up onto the gallery could get inside his room and wait for him to show up.

He thought it extremely likely that this was precisely what Devlin and Red Bandanna had done.

He backed away from the window, straightened to his full height and threw his hat back on. Two in his room, one out back holding the horses for the getaway. It made sense.

Grim-faced now, he crept back along the hallway, wincing every time a loose board groaned beneath his weight. He stopped just before he reached his own door and, holding his breath, leaned past the frame so that he could put his ear close to one of the panels.

He stayed like that for three full minutes, listening but hearing only the faint street-sounds that drifted up from outside.

Then–

Someone on the other side of the door sniffed wetly.

Chase stood back and let his breath go in a soft hiss. There was no longer any doubt about it, then. They were in there all right, the bushwhacking bastards, and it was unlikely that they'd come all this way just to make peace with him.

If a man can be as cold as ice and fighting mad at the same time, that's how Chase was in that moment. Knowing there was nothing to be gained by delaying the inevitable, he drew his .44, stepped away from the wall, brought one leg up and kicked the flimsy door hard.

It splintered inwards as he threw himself

back out of the line of fire, and the curses of two startled men were quickly followed by a wild, ear-splitting volley of gun-thunder.

Bullets from a handgun peppered the wall facing the doorway, but they were as nothing to the deeper, vicious boom of the twin shotgun blasts that chewed the faded floral wallpaper out of all recognition.

Muttering a few choice cuss-words of his own, Chase dropped to a crouch and threw himself low into the doorway. He caught a brief glimpse of Devlin and Red Bandanna in the weak hallway lamplight, saw that they'd been standing at the foot of his bed, Devlin already breaking open a long-barrelled, smoking Loomis IXL No 15 shotgun so that he could feed in fresh rounds, Red Bandanna still fanning his .38 as if he were so keyed-up that he didn't know when or how to stop.

Having seen all he needed to, Chase loosed a rapid series of gunshots into the semi-darkness.

His first two bullets smashed into Red Bandanna's chest and shoved him back against the bedstead, and even as he bounced off the polished brasswork and fell to the carpet, Chase was throwing himself sideways, beneath the sudden, sodden gush of his blood.

He landed on one shoulder, rolled and came up on the far side of the bed, still triggering the Colt, but by now the shattered door had swung shut again and plunged them all back into near-darkness.

Pandemonium filled the room. Red Bandanna was squirming around and yelling, *'Gimme light, somebody! Don't let me go in the dark!'* Ignoring him, Chase flattened to the thin carpet as Devlin, having reloaded the shotgun, promptly emptied it at him again.

Double-ought shot riddled a nearby chest of drawers and shattered the chamber set that sat atop it, sending splinters of wood and shards of china everywhere. Chase came up over the feather mattress but ducked again when Devlin rose as a silhouette against the window and threw the empty weapon at him.

The shotgun sailed harmlessly overhead, but it bought Devlin enough time to hurl

197

himself back out through the opened window and onto the gallery overlooking the street.

Desperately Chase fired the Colt again. The window-panes exploded but by then Devlin was out of sight, and Chase could hear the slam-slam-slam of his boots as he raced away.

He came up, leapt over the bed and surged after him, dived through the window, rolled and slammed sharp against an ornate white railing five feet away. Midway along the gallery Devlin turned, dropped, and Chase saw that he'd drawn his handgun.

The weapon barked twice, and splinters flew up just inches from Chase's face. Flinching, he powered up onto one knee, threw another shot at Devlin, missed, worked the trigger again, but–

'Damn!'

The gun was empty.

Streetlight showed Devlin legging it to the far corner of the gallery and climbing over the railing, and all Chase could do was stand there and watch him go.

He thought, *Oh yeah?*

He knew where Devlin was headed – back along the alley towards Silver Studs and his waiting horse. So–

Moving quickly, he flipped open the Colt's loading gate, notched back the hammer and turned the cylinder. Empty shell-cases tinkled against the boards at his feet. As he climbed back through the window, he was already thumbing reloads from his belt and stuffing them into the empty chambers, working by feel and the surety that comes with a lifetime of practice.

The room was quiet now, which meant that Red Bandanna was either dead or in shock. He figured the former was more likely than the latter. He leapt over the body and tore open the fragmented door. The minute he appeared in the hallway, pale, curious faces were hastily drawn back into the adjoining rooms. He paid them no mind, just ran the length of the hallway and wrenched open the window at the far end.

As he threw himself out onto the fire stairs, he saw Silver Studs peering up at him, still fighting to control the horses, who were acting edgier still now, because of all the gunfire.

The man called up uncertainly, 'Al?'

Chase called back, 'Nope.'

Silver Studs swore and let go the reins so that he could bring his right hand down to the weapon at his hip.

Chase shot him twice, once in the chest, once in the throat, and Silver Studs gurgled sickly and back-pedaled until he struck the plank wall behind him, then corkscrewed to earth. The horses, meanwhile, lurched away from him and started spilling back along the alley with their loose reins flapping around them like crazy leather snakes.

Chase took the fire stairs three at a time, hit dirt at the bottom and went blurring past the dead man even as a sudden, horrified screech cut through the night air and came pretty close to freezing the blood in his veins.

Immediately he broke stride, and more warily now, followed his gun-barrel around the corner, into the shadowy side-alley. He saw at once that the alley was empty, the horses having exploded out onto Main and gone their own terrified way, and slowed to a halt, breathing hard, wondering where the scream had come from, what it meant, whether or not Devlin had been responsible for it.

After the violence, everything in the side-alley seemed quiet and still. As his pulses settled, Chase started edging carefully toward the lights of Main, eighty feet away.

He'd gone about five paces when he heard a soft groan, and realized that what he'd first taken to be a bundle of rags thrown carelessly up against the wall was in fact a man.

More precisely, it was Devlin.

Quickly he knelt beside the man, reached a hand to his shoulder and turned him onto his back. Devlin rolled over loosely, the movement turning his groan into a howl of agony. As near as he could see in the poor light, Devlin had been chopped and broken in a hundred different places. His pocked, spiteful face was slick with blood. One blue eye was puffed shut, the other glaring up at him from out of a puddle of torn skin. The man's nose was broken, his lips split, chest caved in. His breathing was a shuddery, laboured rasp.

Suddenly Chase understood the significance of the scream. Having dropped from the gallery, Devlin had raced along the alley, determined to reach his mount and get away. Instead of that, however, he'd run smack into the horses, who'd been galloping at him from the opposite direction. The animals had cannoned into him, and their flailing hooves had ripped him apart.

At last Devlin stopped moaning and tried to say something but couldn't. Chase frowned at him, trying to guess what it was. Devlin's single eye swivelled in the direction of the gun in Chase's fist and somehow he reached out to grasp Chase's wrist with a hand that was bruised and broken and more like a claw. His mangled lips worked again, and Chase leaned forward, the better to hear him.

Devlin said, '...'*m beggin*'...'

Chase looked at him again, and somehow

Devlin found the strength to nod, just a little. He was dying and the agony of his injuries was too much for him to stand. Much as he hated and wanted to kill Chase, he wanted Chase to put him out of his misery.

The Spurlock gun said, 'I did as much for your brother, Devlin. Reckon you can understand why, now.'

But even as he finished speaking and steeled himself to do as the man had asked, the life drained from that one staring eye and Devlin's final breath left him in a low, awful rattle.

'All right, drop the gun!'

Chase tore his eyes away from the dead man, identified Tom Fry's silhouette against the lights of Main Street. Now that the gunfight was over, rubber-neckers were starting to gather behind him and line the boardwalk on the other side of the street. The hotel clerk was standing right behind the marshal, an old rifle in his fists.

'It's okay, marshal,' he called back tiredly. 'It's me.'

Recognizing his voice, Fry came hustling down to him. 'You all right, Donovan?' he asked, stopping when he caught sight of Devlin. 'Ho-ly Jesus…'

Chase gestured vaguely. 'I'm fine. But you'll find another body around yonder corner, and a third one in my room.'

'What in tarnation happened? You reckon them North Towners–'

'It's a long story,' Chase cut in. 'But it's got nothing to do with North Town. This was personal.'

He felt Fry squinting at him. 'You sure you're all right, son?'

'Yeah. Could use a cup o' coffee, though.'

The lawman clapped him on one shoulder. 'Come on, I got some cookin' right across the way, there,' he replied. 'I'll have some fellers clean this mess up, an' then you can tell me all about it.'

It was a little after nine o'clock when Chase left the marshal's office and headed back to the hotel. The clerk was still looking pasty-faced at the events of the evening, but he recovered himself long enough to tell Chase that all his gear had been transferred to Jonah's room, until they could fix the window and get the bloodstains out of the carpet.

Chase took his new key and went upstairs, let himself into the room and pulled the curtains before striking a match and lighting the lamp. He felt worn-out, still a little shaky from the earlier violence. When he glanced at the bed, however, he saw that his gear had been laid out on the mattress – and so had Devlin's discarded shotgun.

He reached for the weapon, hefted it, broke it open and ejected the spent cartridges, then snapped it shut again and thumbed back the curved hammer. The piece had a good, solid action and a balance that impressed him, so he decided to hang onto it. Devlin sure wasn't going to need it any more.

As he cleared his stuff off the bed and sat down on the edge of the mattress so that he could finally drag off his boots and sleep the

rest of the night away, he suddenly remembered the envelope the clerk had given him
before all hell'd busted loose.

He drew it from his pocket, tore it open
and extracted a single sheet of neat
copperplate which read:

Mr Donovan,
I should like to speak with you on a most
delicate matter, and would be obliged if you
would call upon me at any time this
evening. Trusting that I may rely upon your
circumspection in this matter, I remain,
Respectfully yours,
Emily McNair.

She gave an address on Third Street.

Chase re-read the note and wondered if it
was bait to lure him into another trap.
Could be. But if it was genuine, why did the
girl want to see him? Either way, there was
only one way to find out.

He got up, reached for his hat and turned
out the lamp. Ten minutes later he was

standing in the shadows across the road from a line of neat clapboard houses fronted by small dirt yards that were enclosed by low picket fences, checking on the lay of the land. Emily MacNair's place was easy to spot: it was the only house where plants and flowers seemed to proliferate.

The night had turned chilly now, and Willow Bend was mostly in darkness, although a light still burned behind Emily's drawn curtain, and North Town was still making plenty of noise.

He waited for fifteen minutes before he decided it was safe to go over. Then he peeled away from the shadows, crossed the street, let himself through Emily MacNair's gate and walked up to the door. He stood to one side of the portal before knocking, just in case, but this time the night didn't explode with gun-thunder. In fact, nothing at all happened for about thirty seconds, and then the door opened and Emily MacNair peered outside.

'Mr Donovan?' she asked in a whisper.

He dipped his head. 'I'm sorry for the lateness of the hour, ma'am, but–'

She didn't let him finish, just opened the door a little wider and told him to come inside. He did so and when she'd closed and bolted the door after her, she led him into a small but comfortable parlour, where an elderly couple sat worriedly on the edge of a faded horsehair sofa.

'Mama, papa,' she said. 'This is the man I was telling you about.'

Chase took off his hat and nodded to the couple. Emily's father stood up and offered his hand. He was tall and thin, with a long face and iron-grey hair. 'Understand you had some trouble tonight, Mr Donovan,' he remarked soberly. 'Whole town's buzzin' with it.'

Chase shook with him, then turned his attention to the girl. 'I got your note,' he said. 'Came as soon as I was able. What's this, ah, "delicate matter" you wanted to discuss, ma'am?'

She gestured that he should take a chair

on the other side of the homely room. As he lowered himself into it, the lamplight showed him a pale, restless young girl with a worried twist to her full lips.

'Rumour has it that you're here to clean up North Town,' she said, and there was a little flutter in her tone. 'Is that why you called on Mr Van Outen this morning?'

He shrugged, not sure how much he could afford to give away.

'Do you have reason to believe that Mr Van Outen is … involved, in any way, with North Town?' she persisted.

'No.'

'Well you *should*,' she replied, and suddenly her manner hardened. 'Because he *is*. He's in it right up to the *neck*.'

Chase eyed her in some surprise. 'You got anything to back that up?' he asked.

Her well-spaced blue eyes dropped away from his, and she wrung her hands in frustration. 'No. Only what I suspect.' The eyes came back to his face, and there was something earnest in them now, a desperate need to be believed. 'I have worked for Mr Van Outen for two years,' she said. 'And never once in all that time has he ever taken me into his full confidence. But I have eyes and ears, Mr Donovan. I see and hear things that make me wonder if he is everything he claims to be.'

'Such as?'

'He banks his money regularly here in town, which of course is sound business practice. But he has additional accounts in Durango, and deposits large amounts into each every two weeks.'

'What does that prove?' he countered. 'Perhaps he feels safer, keeping part of his money in a bigger town.'

'That may be the case,' she agreed. 'But surely he is putting his money at considerably greater risk, carrying it unescorted across more than eighty miles of open and potentially hostile territory. And in any case, where does he get this additional money? Quite by accident I saw one of his ledgers once, just before he locked it away in the safe. I know quite a bit about the legitimate business he conducts, and it *does not* bring in anywhere near such amounts. Then there are all the "meetings" he attends. Meetings which I do not arrange for him, about which he never speaks, and which never seem to yield any more business for him.'

'What are you saying, then?'

'That he has business interests he chooses neither to declare nor discuss, most probably in North Town. That he banks the money earned from these additional business interests in Colorado because he is anonymous there.'

Chase snorted. 'Maybe you're right,' he allowed. 'But I can understand why he'd keep his involvement with North Town quiet. He's a church-goer, isn't he? Man like that could lose a lot of standing in the community if word got out that he'd invested in a saloon or a … well, some other place of entertainment.'

The angry shake of her head sent a shiver through her auburn curls, and the hiss of

expelled breath summed up her mood per-
fectly. 'I can see that I am wasting your time,
Mr Donovan,' she said stiffly. 'I apologise.
Please allow me to see you to the door.'

He took the hint and climbed to his feet.
'I'm sorry too, Miss MacNair. But what it
all comes down to is proof. If you–'

Suddenly her eyes widened and she said,
'What if you saw his secret ledgers for yourself?'

'I thought you said he keeps them locked
in his safe?'

'He does. But I know the combination. He
doesn't *know* that I know, but I *do*. We could
go now, if you like. I have keys to the office
and I'm not afraid.'

He was tempted, but there was another
reason to tread carefully. With uncharacteristic restraint he pointed out, 'Van Outen
lives above his office, doesn't he?'

Her enthusiasm faded. 'Well, yes. But–'

'Then it's too risky. Unless…'

'Yes?'

'I got a better idea,' he said. 'There's no

need to involve you in this. Give me the keys and the combination and I'll check it out on my own.'

'When?'

He shrugged. 'He'll be going to the meeting tomorrow night, won't he?'

'Well, yes,' she replied. 'But even so, you cannot afford to tarry. You don't know what you're looking for. I *do.*'

He sighed. She was right there. So he turned to Emily's worried parents and said, 'Mr MacNair?'

Her father said slowly, 'I raised a headstrong young lady here, Mr Donovan, and one with no shortage of grit. Furthermore, if she says Van Outen's a snake, I believe her. All I ask is that you look after her while she's in your care.'

Chase nodded and turned back to the girl. 'All right,' he said. 'It's agreed, then. Tomorrow night, we go commit a little larceny. But I only hope you're right, ma'am.'

'I am, Mr Donovan,' she replied forcefully. 'I'm sure I am.'

NINE

Morning in Willow Bend…

Felix Van Outen opened his office door and snapped, 'Miss MacNair. A word, if you please.'

Seated at her desk, Emily looked up from her work just as the Dutchman turned and disappeared back into his room. All at once she felt decidedly uneasy. It was only a little after nine o'clock; what possible reason could he have for wanting to see her so soon after she had arrived for work?

Had he learned about the note she'd left for Mr Donovan, or his subsequent visit to her home? For one insane moment, she even wondered if he could read minds, and had seen what she and Donovan were proposing to do later that same evening.

She stood up, edged around her desk and

went down through the little gate, walking on legs like wooden blocks. Mouth suddenly dry, she hesitated in his doorway, cleared her throat and, struggling to sound normal, said, 'Yes, Mr Van Outen?'

Sometimes, she thought, he could appear so kindly. And whenever that mood was upon him, she wondered how she could possibly suspect him of any dishonesty. It was a silly, romantic notion, but sometimes she felt that, in her, he saw the daughter he had perhaps yearned for but never had.

But that certainly was not the case now. He was standing behind his desk, hands behind his back, the brow above his very pale blue eyes furrowed, and as he glared at her – there was no other word for it – his round, yellowish face appeared almost angry.

She thought, *Oh my God. He knows what I've done.*

But in the next moment the expression softened and he gestured to the poster on his desk and said, 'Be so good as to display this in the front window, if you please, Miss MacNair.'

Her eyelids fluttered with relief, and as her shoulders sagged she nodded eagerly. 'Oh. Yes, Mr Van Outen. Of course.'

He turned away from her and took up the gibus hat and white French gloves that he habitually kept on top of the safe. 'Are you going out, sir?' she asked.

He nodded, face and tone hardening again. 'Yes. I do not propose to be long, but in any case, you have your tasks for the morning.'

'Yes, sir,' she replied meekly, and reached for the poster.

Twenty minutes later, Quintus Ashe reached an empty lot on the westernmost tip of town, checked to make sure no-one else was around, then let himself inside.

He said, 'I came as soon as I received your message. I can guess what it's about.'

Van Outen, standing on the other side of the small, dim room, turned as the mangiant closed the door behind him and his pit bull sat dutifully at his side, its ribs swelling and contracting rapidly in time to its noisy panting.

The property in which they found themselves was small and run-down. Van Outen had purchased it for next to nothing three years earlier for the privacy it afforded him. Personally he found the place distasteful, for though he did not make it as obvious as Ashe, he too was a man who enjoyed the finer things in life. In fact, he had engineered the entire North Town business just so that he would have sufficient funds to indulge his every whim when he finally shook the dust of Willow Bend from his heels.

He said, 'Donovan is still alive.'

Ashe nodded. 'And that's not all. I think we have ourselves a problem here, Felix. To hear the way they tell it, the people are coming to look upon this Donovan as some sort of hero.'

'I know. That is why we will have to deal with him in a far more … subtle … manner.

Through the very man he came here to help – Fry.'

Ashe's brows lowered over his bloodshot eyes. 'It's too early in the day to be talking riddles,' he complained.

'Then I will make myself plain. If we are to be rid of Donovan, we must turn our attention to a considerably … easier … target. Fry's wife.'

'Hey, now,' said Ashe, shaking his head. 'Don't get me wrong. It makes no difference to me whether the woman lives or dies. But having her roughed-up the last time left a bad taste in quite a few mouths, even down in North Town. Target her again and you're just liable to spark off a revolt.'

'Not if we ensure that it is our friend *Dexter* who receives the blame,' Van Outen countered smoothly. 'And that shouldn't be difficult. You know how to spread the word.' He frowned. 'Where is that imbecile, anyway?'

'He lit out yesterday morning. No one's seen him since. But I don't suppose he's gone far. He totes grudges, that one.'

'All the more reason for the townsfolk to believe our little … deception. A grudge-toter, striking back at the man who had him kicked out of office.'

'I still don't understand how getting rid of Fry's wife helps us with Donovan.'

'Fry is not entirely stupid. He'll soon realize that his wife would never have died had he not brought Donovan here in the first place. Therefore, he will dismiss the man rather than put any of his other confederates at risk,' Van Outen explained. 'Do you see what I am saying? He will get rid of Donovan *for* us.'

'You *hope*.'

'I have studied human nature for many years, Ashe. In my business, you have to. Believe me, I *know* how Fry will react.'

'Well,' opined Ashe, 'he'll either do as you say – or he'll send Donovan out to nail our backsides to the wall.'

Van Outen raised one quizzical eyebrow. 'Are you frightened of him?' he asked with faint, grim amusement.

'You know me better than that,' said Ashe, and at his side Jack growled ominously.

Unimpressed, the Dutchman clapped his gibus hat atop his head and pushed his long-fingered hands into his white gloves. 'Well, see to it. And if it makes you feel any happier, arrange it so that your hired thugs attack the old Mills place while you and I are in plain sight at this infernal meeting tonight.'

Ashe nodded. 'All right. But I hope to God you really *do* know what you're doing, Felix, because if you don't, this entire business is just likely to blow up right in our faces.'

High noon in Willow Bend…

Chase sat at a corner table in the café, just drinking coffee and thinking. He'd risen early, washed, shaved, dressed and strolled down to the eaterie, knowing that he had a long day ahead of him.

He wasn't really sure what to make of

Emily MacNair's suspicions, but she'd struck him as being sincere, and that alone had made him curious enough to want to take a look at the contents of Felix Van Outen's safe for himself. Trouble was, he still had to wait the best part of half a day before they could meet up and do just that, and waiting had never been his strong point.

Hell, he told himself wryly, just ask Captain Taylor.

But as he drank more coffee and mulled over all kinds of random thoughts just to pass the time, he came to realize that something strange had happened to him ever since he'd signed on with Andrew Spurlock. He'd started acting and thinking more like a lawman and less like some Biblical avenger.

And damn, if the change didn't agree with him.

That's why, instead of busting in on Van Outen and getting the man to open his safe at gunpoint, and maybe losing the girl her job and making himself look a fool in the process, he just sat and drank coffee and actually *waited*.

Slowly, slowly, the afternoon wore on.

Mid-afternoon in Willow Bend…

At the municipal hall, Tom Fry, John Setright and Ernie Weems started setting out row upon row of hard wooden benches, each one lined up in front of a low dais, upon which the principal speakers would state the case for the new town ordinances later that evening.

And as evening finally came out at the old Mills place…

'More coffee, Mr Kissing?'

Jonah shook his head and slapped the stomach beneath his plain blue shirt. 'No thank you, ma'am. Ah reckon this here stitchin's comin' pretty close to bustin' as it is.'

Phoebe Fry, a trim little woman in her middle forties, with a weathered but still handsome face and silky hair the colour of gunmetal gathered in a bun at the back of her head, took that as a compliment and positively beamed at him in the dull, smoky light of the Argant lamp that was set on the table between them.

'Well,' she said, rising to gather up the crockery, 'you been so kind, coming out here to watch over me and set Tom's mind at rest. I guess I just want to make you feel at home.'

'You shore done that, ma'am,' he assured her. 'But they's no need t'go fussin' over me. Ah'm jus' doin' a job is all.'

He'd arrived mid-morning the day before, to be greeted by the dark barrel of a rifle showing in the half-open kitchen doorway and a stern voice calling, *'That's far enough! Get your hands up and state your business!'*

Once he'd convinced the woman of his good intentions, and she'd read the note of introduction her husband had written her, she'd set her long-gun aside and greeted him like a long-lost son. 'Fact, she'd been treating him that way ever since, even though she was only five or six years older than him.

Now he stood up, eased the knots in his spine and reached for his grey Stetson, the evening meal of pork chops, eggs and cracklin' bread settling nicely inside him. Full dark was just minutes from claiming the open country to the west of Willow Bend now, and shadows were filling the brokendown but patched-up kitchen despite the meagre lamplight.

Now that he came to think on it, they'd spent most of their time in the kitchen, which was the most habitable room on the old, abandoned ranch. Phoebe Fry liked to cook, and she was almighty good at it. She was also a strong, friendly woman, and it had angered him to see the marks of so many fading bruises on her pleasant face and think about what Dexter had done to her.

As he headed for the door, he slid his Winchester from its sheath in the corner and pumped the lever. 'Think Ah'll jus' take a li'l stroll around the property, ma'am,' he said.

Turning from the range, she ran floury hands down the white apron she wore over her sensible Princess dress and noted, 'You sure do take your work seriously, Mr Kissing.'

'Ah like to take a pride in whut Ah do,' he allowed.

'Well, don't be long. I'm just through baking one of my special apple and cinnamon pies. You hurry back and get some while it's hot.'

He smiled at her. 'Ah shore will, ma'am.'

As he unlatched the door and stepped outside, a gunshot blasted at him from the darkness on the other side of yard.

He dropped flat as splinters gouged from the door-frame hit him in the left cheek and set the side of his face a-burning. Behind him, Phoebe Fry loosed off a scream and he yelled, *'Grab yo'self some cover, ma'am! An' put the lamp out!'*

A volley of gunblasts – pistols, he thought, not long-guns – chewed more wood out of the door-frame, and he told himself he must've surprised whoever was out there before they could creep up on the house.

He started bellying back into the kitchen, screwing his heavy-lidded, flake-gold eyes shut so that they'd adjust to the darkness that much sooner. When he opened them again, the kitchen was filled with shadow. Good – Phoebe'd seen to the lamp.

At last the fusillade ended. 'You awright, ma'am?' he called softly, without looking around.

'Y-yes. But who–?'

Before she could finish the question, he saw a shadow break from the bigger block of shadow that was the barn, and slapped the Winchester's cold stock up to his cheek.

The shadow raced across the yard. He made out a man holding something heavy and oblong-shaped in one hand. The man was heading for the tumbledown bunk-house, which made him think, *Sumbitches're fixin' to out-flank us.*

He tracked the running man, let him get maybe twenty yards, then swept the weapon a little ahead of him and squeezed the trigger. The Winchester jolted and the man ran straight into the bullet. Jonah saw him haul up as if he'd just run smack into an invisible wall, and then he dropped whatever it was he'd been carrying and he twisted and fell and didn't move again.

Even as the man went down, though, two of his friends – all Jonah could see were silhouettes in big hats, also carrying hefty containers – made their move, one heading for the far end of the main house, the other trying to cross that killing ground to reach either the bunkhouse or the wagon-shed.

Jonah came up onto one knee, worked the action, sighted on the second man and blew the bastard's brains out.

He worked the lever again, brought the Winchester around – but froze. There was no sign of the other one.

That meant he'd made it to the house.

Damn!

He called softly, 'Ma'am…'

She worked the lever of her own rifle by

way of reply, and whispered, 'Don't worry. If he shows his face on this side of the house, I'll send him to hell in a handcart.'

A short, tight smile worked his thick lips. She had grit, this woman. Then he put his eyes back on the yard and the smile died. Two bodies out there, just pools of darkness against the rutted hardpan. A third man creeping around somewheres off to the right. Any more? He thought, *Jesus, if they's carryin' what I* think *they's carryin'*...

He hated the notion of just kneeling here and waiting for them to do their worst. So...

Cautiously he rose to his feet, and holding the Winchester across his broad chest, edged back outside. Only the snorting and stamping of the scared horses in the barn broke the heavy night silence. He waited a while. Nothing happened, except that he thought he heard some faint kind of water-spilling noise that made his skin go cold.

Gripping the Winchester a little tighter, and keeping his back to the plank and mud-plaster wall, he started light-footing towards the far corner of the dwelling, moving faster now, because–

He caught it then, a smell carrying on the faint breeze, and it confirmed his growing suspicions.

He thought, *Aw, Christ – kerosene.*

And hard on the heels of that: *That's whut them other fellers wuz totin'. They goan try to burn us alive, or shoot us down when we try to make a run fo' it.*

Even as the thought skewered his brain, a dull *crumping* sound slapped through the darkness, and he knew that he was too late to do anything to stop it, that the man who'd made it to the far side of the house had already doused the place in oil and put a match to it.

He broke away from the wall, made a wild run for the end of the house, came around the corner with the Winchester braced against his hip and almost ran straight into the fire.

As he made a clumsy backwards lurch to escape the searing heat, he saw that the side-wall was already burning fiercely, that the flames were spreading fast because the house was old, dry, a death-trap.

Then he caught the briefest glimpse of a man on the far side of the fire-wall – husky, clad in a sheepskin jacket, lower face covered by a bandanna, the rest of his face shadowed by the brim of his big hat.

The man hurled his empty kerosene can at Jonah and Jonah threw himself sideways and slammed against the trampled, weedy earth. He rolled, expecting the man to follow the can with a bullet, most likely more than one, and he wasn't disappointed. The man drew a Colt from beneath his jacket and sent two fast shots at him. Jonah came up, brought the stock of the Winchester to his cheek and fired, levered, fired back. The man dodged out of sight around the back of the house and cussing a blue streak, Jonah powered up and after him.

Giving the oil-fed flames a wide berth, he made it to the corner just as the other man, already halfway along the back of the house, turned at the waist and fired at him again without breaking stride. Jonah returned fire once, twice, three times, but the light here was poor and the target was moving real fast.

The other man emptied his sixgun in Jonah's direction and Jonah dodged behind a stack of chopped wood. He waited for several seconds, until he was sure the other man wasn't going to throw any more shots at him, then came around the woodpile and started chasing back the way he'd come.

The yard was considerably brighter by now, the spreading fire casting a fitful orange light that chased the darkness away. Jonah came back around the house just in time to see the other man zig-zagging towards the barn, beyond which he and his friends had likely tethered their mounts.

He fired at the man and cursed when he missed again. Then, in a moment of inspiration, he switched aim, focused on the can of kerosene that was still lying on one side next to the first man he'd shot. Pausing just long enough to send up a quick prayer, he pulled the trigger and the can exploded in a roaring burst of white light, spilling liquid flame up and out in a wide, breathtaking arc.

The startled fire-lighter froze in his tracks, hunched his shoulders and clapped his arms over his head in order to protect himself from the fiery shower, and while he was like that, Jonah snap-aimed and drilled him once, twice, three times, and the man was flung off his feet to land in a lifeless heap six feet away.

Jonah let his breath out in a low, tired sigh and looked around. The burning house and the smaller fire still burning in the centre of the yard were sending twin beacons of light out across the lonely prairie, but he didn't figure there was anyone else left out there to see it. He hurried to the kitchen door, yelling Phoebe's name, and a moment later the woman came running out, her apron and skirt gathered up in one hand, the other still folded around her rifle.

They stood side by side a safe distance

from the house and watched it burn. The fire was already so advanced that there was nothing they could do to stop it. Smoke thickened rapidly and rose skyward to blot out the stars and moon above. The heat was tremendous.

Tears slid wetly down the woman's smoke-darkened face, as the horses stamped and snorted restlessly in the barn behind them. At length she said ironically, 'Where do I hide now, Mr Kissing?'

She looked so forlorn that he felt his anger building all over again. 'You don't,' he replied, reaching a decision. 'You' all through hidin', Mrs Fry.'

'But–'

'You an' me is goin' back to town now,' he told her. 'An' when we git there, Ah'm goan settle with whoever set this thing up so you won't never have t'hide *again*.'

'You don't have to go through with this, you know,' said Chase.

Emily MacNair, clad in a fetching Eton

jacket, looked up at him as they hustled through the near-deserted town, headed for Van Outen's office. It was a little after seven o'clock in the evening, and the meeting at the municipal building was finally starting to get underway. 'I know,' she replied. 'But *if* I am right, and by proving it we can bring all this terrible trouble with North Town to an end, then the risk is worth it.'

He made no reply, but again he found himself pondering his changing attitudes. Not so long ago, he'd held a pretty low opinion of damn'-near everyone. But ever since he'd met up with Jonah and the Spurlocks, he'd come to realize that maybe he'd been a little too eager to misjudge folks. In truth, most people weren't so bad, provided you made the effort to get to know 'em. He'd never really done that – until now.

Five minutes' hurried walking finally brought them to Van Outen's office. At Chase's insistence, they paused in the alley where he and Jonah had spied on Phil Dexter the night before, just to check the place out. It was in darkness.

'You ready?' he asked.

Emily's response was a determined nod.

'All right,' he said, starting across the quiet road. 'Let's get to it.'

They climbed onto the far boardwalk and Emily took a set of keys from her reticule. While she opened up the office, Chase kept lookout. As the door swung open, the bell on the frame above it tinkled with a sound that was magnified out of all proportion by the night silence, and it was all he could do to stifle a curse.

They slipped inside and the girl closed and locked the door behind them. Chase listened to the place, straining for any sound that would tell him for certain whether or not the building was occupied. He heard her breathing, his, the ticking of a yellow-faced wall-clock, but that was all.

The office smelled vaguely citrusy. That would be her precious plants, Chase told himself as he followed her through the little gate and up to the door of Van Outen's private office.

She opened the door and they went inside. Only when they were crouched together in front of the Jenks & Millbush safe behind the Dutchman's desk did he chance scratching a match to life. They traded a look in its restless flicker, and the girl, chewing at her bottom lip now, looked very young.

He whispered, 'All right – open 'er up.'

She went to work with one delicate little hand, spinning the dial one way, then the other. Click after click filled the poky office, and then she reached for the brass handle above the dial and turned it hard towards the ceiling.

Chase shook out the spent match and shoved it into his pocket, knowing better than to leave any incriminating evidence behind him, then struck another and reached past her to haul the door open. Inside he saw a neat stack of documents, each tied in dark ribbon, a small strong-box and a pile of ledgers.

'These?' he asked, indicating the books.

She nodded and he reached inside to draw them out.

He had to strike a third match before he could start scanning them, and at first all he saw was column after column of crabbed, seemingly meaningless figures.

'I'll say one thing for your boss,' he observed sourly as one fruitless minute melted into another. 'He sure believes in keeping detailed records.'

He struck another match, turned and scanned another page, but when the figures still didn't make any sense, he set the book aside with ill-concealed impatience and reached for another, asking, 'What do *you* make of it?'

She shook her head, her expression vexed. 'I'm just not sure, other than that he appears to have several different sources of income, none of which are linked to his legitimate business activities.'

When she put it that way, everything started making a crazy kind of sense to him. Hastily he reached for the ribbon-tied documents, fumbled one open and read it through quickly.

Beside him, the girl whispered eagerly, 'What is it?'

He refolded the document, said grimly, 'It's rope, Miss Emily.'

He felt her eyes on him. 'Rope?' she repeated.

He nodded. 'Well,' he told her, 'let's put it another way. It's gonna hang Van Outen, nothin' surer.'

TEN

Chase waited for Emily to lock Van Outen's office up behind them, then said, 'Best you get on home now, girl.'

Even in the low streetlight he saw her look of surprise. 'Go–? But–'

'No telling which way Van Outen's gonna jump when I brace him,' he told her grimly. 'I'd hate for you to be there if he turns ugly.'

She saw the sense in that and nodded reluctantly. 'All right. But… You'll come by later, to tell me what happened?'

'Sure I will.'

'Take care, then, Mr Donovan.'

They split up and Chase headed for the municipal hall. As he turned the corner into Main, however, a sharp, whistle cut through the night and brought him around. Two riders were walking their horses along the main drag. A moment later he recognized Jonah – which meant that the handsome-looking woman beside him had to be the marshal's wife.

He hurried back to meet them, only noticing their smoke-darkened clothes as he came nearer. 'What happened?' he asked urgently.

Folding his big arms across his saddle-horn, Jonah told it all in a few sentences, finishing with, 'Figgered it was about time them North Towners learned the error o' their ways, Chase.'

'I'm with you there, brother. But maybe you'd better hear what I got to say first.'

'I'm listenin'.'

Chase shook his head. 'Let's get on up to the municipal hall. I don't want to have to say it twice.'

Exchanging a glance, Jonah and Phoebe dismounted and tethered their horses to the nearest rack. Then the three of them headed for a large frame structure partway along the next block, where lights blazed in every thick-glass window.

Chase hustled up the wide stone steps, shoved open one of the two main doors and strode into the big, packed hall beyond. A wall of noise slapped him in the face, as maybe a hundred or more discordant voices joined together in heated debate.

The Spurlock gun took in the scene at a glance. Fry, Setright, Ernie Weems and Bert the blacksmith were seated at a long table on a dais at the other end of the hall, trying to shout down their unruly audience. Setright was banging a gavel in a vain attempt to bring order to the proceedings.

A few heads turned as the newcomers let the door bang shut behind them, and a whisper rippled through the crowd as folks recognized Phoebe Fry. Paying them no mind, Chase started striding along the aisle between benches, Jonah and Phoebe quickly falling into step behind him. Gradually, as more and more heads turned, the sounds of disagreement began to subside. Up on the dais, the marshal stopped yelling too, his eyes going big when he identified his wife.

By the time the three of them stepped up onto the dais, absolute silence filled the meeting-place.

As Tom Fry took his wife in his arms and she assured him in hushed tones that she was fine, Chase turned and looked out at the sea of faces arrayed before him. Overwhelmingly the audience was made up of men, but there was a goodly number of women among their ranks. He figured the split between townsfolk and North Towners was roughly half and half.

At last he said, 'Some of them North Towners was really busy tonight. They tried to burn the marshal's wife out of the place where she's been hiding ever since two others beat her up. Well, they're dead now, them three brave souls. I guess they learned the hard way that crime doesn't pay.'

Another murmur ran through the crowd. One townsman, braver than the rest, stood up and shouted, 'I say we've taken enough from them North Town bullies! Let's burn *them* out!'

There were a few sounds of approval from the people around him, as well as a restless, warning stir among the North Towners gathered on the other side of the hall.

'There'll be none of that!' yelled Chase, and as one they fell quiet again. 'And I'll tell you why. Because you people got no real argument with the North Towners. Most of 'em'd be happy enough to pay their taxes and abide by your laws.

'But there's one man among 'em who stands to lose more than the rest, because he owns pretty close to half the businesses down there. *He's* the man who's been stirring up all the opposition in North Town, getting the folks down there to fight the ordinances for him.'

'Who is he, this man?' asked another towner.

'He's the man who's spent the last few years buying up a saloon here, a cat-house there, always on the quiet,' Chase replied. 'He's the man who's signed every deed he's got with a false name, to keep his own identity secret. And that's not all.'

He waited a moment, deliberately letting the tension build as row after row of faces stared back at him, hanging on his every word. 'He's real greedy, this man. He wasn't satisfied with all the money he was making on the side. He wanted more. So he organized a protection racket to keep the rest of North Town, the part he doesn't already *own,* in line.

'Trouble is, he kept records of every dirty cent he's ever dragged in. So I guess he wasn't as clever as he thought he was.'

'Give us his name!' yelled the first man. 'We'll string the bastard up!'

'There'll be no mob justice here!' bellowed Fry.

Chase nodded. 'The marshal's right!' he called down to them. 'Because I'm gonna arrest the sonofabitch *myself.*'

He stepped down off the dais and started back along the aisle, and right at the back, cringing on the end of a bench, his round, yellowish face drained of blood, Felix Van

Outen watched him come.

Chase said, 'It's all over, Van Outen.' And as his eyes shuttled to the far end of the same bench, he added, 'For you too, Ashe.'

The silence was absolute now, as every head turned to witness the arrest. Just as Chase closed the last few yards toward the Dutchman, however, the double doors suddenly slammed open and someone screamed, *'No you don't you sonofabitch!'*

Phil Dexter stood in the doorframe, his face a sweaty, flushed mask of anger and hatred. He was holding one of his fancy .38s in his right hand, and in the bandaged left he clutched the neck of a whiskey bottle.

No sooner had he finished yelling than the gun in his fist thundered. Women screamed and men yelled and all at once people were scrambling to get out of the line of fire.

Something punched into Chase and he hunched up, his legs turned to jelly and he collapsed, and up on the dais Phoebe Fry screamed and Jonah thought, *Oh my Gawd, no, Dexter's kilt him.*

In the next moment another gun roared, and Jonah's head kind of twitched around as Marshal Fry fanned his .45 twice more. There was more screaming and shouting, and then Dexter was slammed hard against the still-open doors, where he hung suspended for a long few seconds, then slid floorwards and left an ugly red smear on the wood behind him.

Panicky towners started filling the doorway in their haste to escape from all the gunplay, and within seconds Jonah was down there among them, shoving and pushing until he reached Chase.

He knelt, rolled Chase over, said urgently, 'You awright, brother? Speak to me, dammit!'

Chase looked up at him, right hand holding his left shoulder, the fingers stained with blood, green eyes glazed a little with pain. Forcing a nod, he said, 'I'll live. Just … get me back on my feet.'

The effort to rise left him feeling dizzy, but he was feeling good and mad too, and it was the madness in him kept him from falling flat on his face. As Fry, Setright and the others gathered around them, Chase scanned the now nearly-deserted hall, saw that Van Outen and Ashe had disappeared along with the crowd and said, 'Come on, brother – let's go wrap this business up once and for all.'

Palming their Colts, they hustled past Dexter's slowly stiffening body and down the stone steps into the empty street, where they paused for a moment to try and out-think their opponents.

'Where'd you reckon they went, Chase?' whispered Jonah.

The answer to that was, *Not far.* But even as Chase opened his mouth to say as much, he caught a blur of movement from the corner of his eye and spun towards it just as Jack, Ashe's pit bull, came snarling towards them from the shadows of an alley on the other side of the street, jagged teeth bared.

Chase brought his .44 up and fired the weapon once. A spray of dirt no more than two or three feet in front of him halted the animal in its tracks, and with a yelp, it turned tail and ran in the opposite direction.

'Just like its master,' Chase muttered, disdainfully. 'All piss and wind.'

A gunblast rang out then, chipping stone splinters from the steps behind them, and Chase leapt for the cover of a nearby water-trough as a big figure – Ashe – suddenly broke from the cover of the alley and went lumbering up the street after his dog.

Without stopping to think about it, Jonah went surging after him, closed the distance fast and tackled him around the waist. The pair of them went crashing to the ground and the impact jolted Jonah's ivory-handled .45 from his grasp.

At once the two men leapt back to their feet and, because Ashe never carried a gun, started trading punches. Chase came up and around the trough, more intent on collaring Van Outen. Even before he reached the mouth of the alley, however, another gunblast spat orange flame at him and he dropped to a crouch and emptied his pistol into the shadows all around it.

A high scream tore from the darkness, and a moment later the Dutchman staggered out into the light, hugging himself tight, his little handgun hanging loosely by its trigger-guard on one finger.

Chase came up slowly, knowing it was all over, and shoved the empty Colt away as Van Outen stumbled another few paces, then turned on one heel and went down.

A wave of nausea washed through him and he reached back up to hold his throbbing shoulder. When his vision cleared again, he saw Jonah standing above Ashe, bent slightly at the waist and holding his groin.

As Chase walked slowly up to him, Jonah said painfully, 'That Ashe, he di'n't fight me fair. Sumbitch hit me right here, below th' belt. So whut could Ah do but repay the man in kind?'

'Well,' Chase replied around a quirky smile. 'Don't rub 'em, brother. *Count* 'em.'

Jonah chuckled his low, infectious laugh

and turned to the townsmen assembled on the steps outside the municipal hall. 'Marshal,' he called. 'Ah make that one fo' th' undertaker an' another fo' yo' cells.'

Marshal Fry trotted over, handgun still in his fist as, on the ground, Ashe started to regain consciousness. 'All right, big man,' he rasped, nudging Ashe with the tip of one boot. 'Get up, and no more runnin'. You're under arrest.'

A new, clean morning in Willow Bend...

'Well,' said John Setright, 'I know when I'm wrong about a man, and I was certainly wrong about you two. You've done us a real service here, and we're beholden.'

He held out his hand and Chase shook with him. A moment later Jonah did likewise. Setright and his fellow town councillors were gathered together in Chase's hotel room, where Chase himself was stretched out in bed, stripped to the waist but with his shoulder heavily bandaged.

What with one thing and another, it had

been a long night, and he'd spent most of it under the influence of laudanum, while Willow Bend's only doctor worked hard to dig Dexter's bullet out of him. Now he was still feeling a little light-headed, and the shoulder was as sore as a bitch, but he had a feeling that Emily MacNair would be stopping by now that she no longer had a regular job to occupy her, just to fuss over him while he recovered, and he was kind of looking forward to it.

'I got a feelin' North Town'll be a whole lot more settled without Van Outen and Ashe to stir it up,' opined Fry. 'Thanks, you fellers. And remember – you stick around as long as you like. The town's real grateful to you, and we want to show it.'

The townsmen filed out and Jonah closed the door after them. When he turned back to Chase, he held up a flimsy sheet of paper. 'Ah wired Mr Spurlock,' he said, 'an' jus' got this reply. He wants us to send him a full report on whut happened here, soon's we can.'

Chase grimaced. 'Paperwork! Aw,' he said, 'I'm not up to writing yet, brother. I just got shot, remember?'

'In you' *left* arm, not the right.'

'Well … we'll work something out.'

Jonah went over to the window and looked out past the gallery to bustling Main Street. 'Somethin' else Mr Spurlock wanted to know.'

'Oh?'

'Yeah. When you fust signed on, you tol' us that you'd see how this job went afore you let us know whether or not you decided to make it permanent.' He turned around again.

'You reached that decision yet, brother?'

Chase swallowed hard. Well, he thought, here it is. Time to come right out with it. He opened his mouth, intending to say that he'd be pushing on, alone, once he was all finished healing. But what he said instead was, 'I reckon I decided a long time back – partner.'

Jonah's teeth flashed in a smile. 'Ah's

kinda hopin' you'd say that.'

Still weakened by the laudanum and loss of blood, Chase suddenly yawned. 'Now get outta here and let me sleep, will you?' he muttered.

'Sho'. But you better heal real quick, Chase. 'Cordin to that wire from Mr Spurlock, they's another little chore he's got lined up fo' us, down along the Mexican border.'

Chase browned. 'What kind of chore?'

'Bunch'a hardcases've taken over a town down that way, been raisin' Ned an' no one knows why.'

Chase's mood soured as the prospect of being nursed back to health by Emily MacNair seemed to grow less and less likely with every passing second. 'Well, let me rest up for today and maybe we'll ride on tomorrow,' he replied. 'I can heal as well in the saddle as I can in a bed – I guess.'

'Sho'.'

Jonah let himself out and Chase closed his eyes. There in the peace of the room, he wondered whether he'd made the right decision or not. Only time – and their next mission – would tell. Of one thing, however, he was certain.

The West really *was* riddled with all manner of owlhoots and renegades … and the Spurlock gun was going to run hotter than Hell before he and Jonah were all through fighting 'em.

The publishers hope that this book has given you enjoyable reading. Large Print Books are especially designed to be as easy to see and hold as possible. If you wish a complete list of our books please ask at your local library or write directly to:

Dales Large Print Books
Magna House, Long Preston,
Skipton, North Yorkshire.
BD23 4ND